Love

for

Christmas

Love for Christmas

A Holiday Romance Anthology

Vista Point Press
Tustin, California USA

Vista Point Press

Love for Christmas

A Holiday Romance Anthology
First Publication, November 2017
First Print Edition, October 2018

ISBN: 978-1-946996-03-9

Set in 11-point Garamond.

Cover image © Smaglov @ Depositphotos
Cover design © Stardance Media
Book design: Steve Friedl

Table of Contents

A Witch for Christmas

by Barb DeLong

Chapter One

"Abby, I've got the perfect frog guaranteed to break the curse." Sam stood in the doorway of Abigail Goodbody's rented Craftsman bungalow, letting in a blast of cold December air. She hipped the door shut and pulled a frog out of an opaque plastic bag.

"Samantha Theodora, tell me you did not kill that poor creature!" Abby stood frozen at the gas stove, her heart in her throat. She held a handful of dried mugwort root over a steaming cauldron.

"Well, not this one." A limp frog with bulging, dead eyes swung crazily by one of its feet from the tips of Sam's fiercely long fingernails.

Abby's fluffy, white cat Endora abandoned a Christmas ball on the floor and raced over to Sam.

"Don't you dare," Abby cried.

Her *familiar* ignored the fierce mental images of severe punishment Abby sent her way. She stood on her hind legs and batted at the dangling critter and sent back her own message. *Want. Want.*

Sam lifted the frog higher. "I bought the thing from Crawley's shop, from his secret stock. Like I said, guaranteed."

"Right." Abby sighed as she sprinkled the root flakes into the brew. She'd known Sam since childhood and little from her saucy friend surprised her anymore. She shooed Endora away before the cat decided to claw her way up Sam's sprayed-on jeans.

"My mother doesn't even list a frog in her spell book." Abby tucked her long hair, limp from the steam, behind her ears. She ran a finger down the lengthy list of ingredients she'd already added under the heading "Breaking a Curse." *Funny how this page is so stained and worn.* Apparently breaking curses was quite a pastime in her mother's day.

"My mother says a frog a day keeps one happy and fey," Sam said.

"That explains a lot." Abby closed her eyes when Sam swung the poor creature over the water and let go with a brief chant and a plop. "Okay, Sam. We've gone through all the curse breakers in the book. If this spell doesn't work, I've only got eight more days until Christmas Eve to find my one true love or I never will."

"Then let's get this done, girlfriend."

Abby clasped Sam's hand in a firm grip, careful to avoid being stabbed by her friend's painted talons. Sam closed her eyes and began to sway back and forth in front of the stove, more for dramatic effect she liked to say, so Abby did the same. Sam joined her in the chant.

"Fire burn and cauldron bubble,
Free me from this nasty trouble.
No need I find love so true,
This curse is gone, this curse is through.
So say we, two as one,
We declare this curse undone."

Abby kept her eyes tightly shut. She concentrated on her body, the blood flowing through her veins, the strong pulse at her neck, the steady thud of her heartbeat. Wicked sorceress Hilda Grimm had told her when the curse was lifted (or hopefully broken in this case) she'd feel its strong, physical manifestations leave her body and know it was done.

"Anything?" Sam asked.

Abby opened her eyes. "Nothing. I still feel as if a shroud, or some kind of sheath is covering my heart."

"Like a condom on a—"

"Very funny. As if we'd know what that feels like." Abby blew out a breath. "If I'd known how obsessed Roald was with me, I'd have, maybe…"

"You let that demented little snot down very gently because that's how you are. Kind."

"Tell Hilda that. She called me terrible names. Said I devastated her son forever."

"Well, the rest of the females back home in Oakville will be forever grateful to you."

Abby smiled, moving to the sink and washing her hands. "And I'm grateful you've helped me with all these spells. To thank you, I'll share my bottle of Cab."

"Not that we need any excuses for wine, but here's another one. Isn't this your six-month anniversary in this house and away from family and foe?"

"It is. Let's celebrate." Abby scooted over to make room at the sink for Sam and her icky frog fingers. For years Abby had longed for her independence from her big, needy family. When Sam bought a chocolate shop many miles away in Mayfield and offered Abby the manager's position, she jumped at the chance. Finally, she had a place of her own in a quaint little town and a responsible job she loved. She could utilize her MBA in a very real way.

If she couldn't either satisfy or break the curse, she'd have no one to grow old with in this wonderful place. No lover. No kids. Was having a fulfilling job and good friends enough? They might have to be, but not having a family of her own would leave a cruel hollow deep in her soul.

"I can't believe it's been almost a year since you were cursed. I wish I could have found you a true love," Sam said, creating a cloud of soap bubbles as she scrubbed her hands.

"Don't forget the 'true love of heart, soul and mind' part."

"I'm trying, but the search might be easier if we had the whole male population to choose from and not just the witches. If only there were a witchmatch dot com, but we're such a secretive lot." Sam made a rude sound. "We need more time than this Christmas Eve. Damn that Hilda Grimm. I'd like to curse her to the devil's pit."

"Well, we can't. Both of us together aren't powerful enough to create a wart on the nose of a sorceress like her."

"She already has one, anyway."

"Huh, you're right. But a matching pair would be perfect."

Through the window over the sink, Abby had a view of the side fence and the house next door. A light went on in the kitchen. Seven o'clock. Joe worked late today.

Sam wore a huge grin that scrunched all the freckles on her face clear up to her cheekbones.

"What," said Abby.

"You. That look on your face when Joe's light went on. All soft with a slight little frown. Eyes aglow."

"Eyes aglow? What have you been reading? Joe's a friend. I worry that he's working too hard, just like I worry about you."

"Hmph. Joe is true-love material."

"If he were a witch. He's an Ordinary. He doesn't have the faery mark on his back. Too bad we can't just sniff the guys and know who's a witch."

Sam closed her eyes and clutched her chest. "If only I'd been here when he took his shirt off for you."

"He didn't take it off for me. The heat was stifling when he fixed the pipe in the bathroom. Definitely not romantic."

Abby remembered the scene as if it were yesterday instead of months ago. Six foot something of rippling muscles, a six-pack of abs, big, strong, capable hands wielding a hefty wrench. No faery mark. That had been so disappointing because Joe was hot. More importantly, he was a really good guy.

"Did you make sure the mark wasn't lower, like on the top of one of his beautiful, hard buttocks?" Sam asked. "You know, plumber, butt crack."

Abby laughed. "No, his jeans were respectably located."

Sam pouted. "Well, phooey. I'd go for him if I didn't already have my Ryan Gosling. Joe wears his heart on his sleeve. Too bad for him that he's fallen for you."

There was really no denying the obvious. Joe had tried for months to take their friendship to the next level. Only finding love with another witch before the deadline would end the curse. Ordinaries were off the table entirely. Love with an Ordinary would end in heartbreak for the both of them. She just couldn't do that to Joe, so Abby had discouraged him every step. Then, a couple of months ago, Joe kissed her. Not just any kiss. A fantastic, flight-to-the-moon-and-back kiss.

Afterwards, she did the hardest thing she'd ever done in her life. She told him she just wanted to remain friends. Tell that to a man who adores you and see how much you hurt him. Her heart still ached at the pain she saw in his eyes. Hilda Grimm would be laughing maniacally if she could see Abby having to do the same thing to someone Abby really cared about as she'd done to Hilda's precious Roald.

After they'd shared a couple of glasses of wine, or three, Sam left. Abby lugged the heavy cauldron to the backyard to bury the contents with the usual ritual. The area behind the house so designated for such secret rites was hidden from view of other homes by high hedges. The ground was littered with small mounds like the burial site of tiny pets. She sighed, vowing to add a few words for the dear froggy who had made the ultimate sacrifice. Then she was going to see what was going on with the irritating itch that had begun on the side of her neck. She was probably having a bad reaction to this latest foul concoction just like last time. Lucky for her immune system that she and Sam were fresh out of spells.

Joe Ganon pulled his work truck into a parking spot directly in front of The Magic of Chocolate at precisely noon. He was hoping Abby would have lunch with him while on her break. He peered across the sidewalk and through the shop window at the same time as setting his clipboard on the passenger seat. He knocked a half-cup of cold coffee out of the holder with the sleeve of his jacket. The odor of stale dark roast filled the cab. Splashes of coffee dripped from the underside of the dash. He wasted the three hours he spent detailing the interior.

"Damn!" *That's what I get for being distracted.* Beautiful Abby "let's-just-be-friends" Goodbody did that to him. *All the time.*

He was tempted to chant a cleanup spell but he'd promised himself he would never use magic like his family did for expediency or laziness. He made his way the honorable, and yes, the hard way. He'd been in Mayfield for three years, keeping his witch identity on the down low to other witches in heavily hocus-pocus Massachusetts. He'd be fine if he never used magic again. He would be only too happy to stifle his powers forever if he could win over Abby because it was never a good idea to come out to an Ordinary. That kind of confession tended to kill relationships.

He thought he caught a glimpse of her in the store. He couldn't help the way his nerves twitched and his pulse quickened whenever he was around her. Or thought about her. Yeah, he had it bad. He kept himself alive remembering that one kiss they'd shared. They'd been on the swing on her front porch. The evening was warm and alive with fireflies, which she said were the souls of departed faeries. She was always saying whimsical stuff like that. He couldn't take his eyes off her. She came by her name honestly—Goodbody. *Hmm.* Next thing, he was kissing her. She had the softest lips. For a few stunning moments, she kissed him back. Then, in her sweet—I-hope-this-won't-hurt—voice, she stabbed him in the heart.

What man stuck around after that "just friends" talk? He would. One day she'd get tired of dating loser after loser trying to find—what? The perfect man? *No such thing, sweetheart.* He vowed to show her that Joe Ganon came as close to perfect as she was gonna get.

He went inside to the tinkling of the bell above the door. The heavy scent of sugar and chocolate made his mouth water and kicked the pleasure center in his brain into overdrive. He liked the Victorian style shop done up in pink and brown stripes with a Christmas-y overlay of evergreen garlands and wreaths. Several small, round tables with fancy wrought-iron chairs were scattered around.

Abby was behind the long, glass counter filled with chocolates and million-calorie éclairs. She looked up from her phone. Her warm smile had his heart banging his ribs like a hammer on an old metal pipe. She wore the store's pink-striped bib apron over a bright pink sweater and an ugly green scarf around her neck. The scarf didn't exactly go with her outfit, but what did he know? Living with three sisters had never helped him figure out a woman's fashion sense. She disappeared through the door to the back room.

Samantha, flaming red hair a crazy halo around her face, stood at the cash register with a cocky grin. "Hi Joe. What can I get you, as if I didn't know?"

Yeah, cocky. "Sam. Just here to see if Abby had her lunch break yet."

"Actually, she's done for the day." She turned her head and yelled. "Abby, Joe wants you for lunch." She arched a brow at him, all cheek and fake innocence.

He groaned. Thank god the couple in the corner were too wrapped up in themselves to take notice. "Thanks a lot. Can you grab us a couple of hot chocolates, please?" Abby wasn't the only reason he loved this place. They served the best coffee in town and apparently, legendary hot chocolate. He decided to switch it up today.

Joe took the table near the window, looped his jacket over the chair back and sat. Abby came out from the storeroom with her coat and purse in hand. He'd cancel his next call if she'd spend the whole afternoon with him. She'd just say no if he asked, so he'd enjoy whatever time he had.

She whispered a few words to Sam, who was adding a foaming mountain of whipped cream to their hot chocolates. Both looked his way. He grinned and waved. Then Abby was slapping Sam's arm. She'd probably said something outrageous because that's how Sam moved.

Abby walked to his table. "Hi, you!" She set her coat and purse on a vacant chair and sat across from him.

Her wide smile lit up her big blue eyes, the exact color of her cat's. She had her long hair tied back in a ponytail. With all that honey-colored hair and cotton candy pink sweater, she looked good enough to eat. Her smile became a grimace as she scratched her neck under the scarf.

"Sorry about lunch, Joe. I ate earlier. But hot chocolate sounds heavenly."

Sam arrived with their steaming mugs. "Here you go, you crazy kids. Enjoy." She winked and left to attend a customer who had just arrived.

He studied Abby's delicate, heart-shaped face as he sipped his drink. "Are you okay? You have redness right—here." He pointed at the blotchiness that came from under the edge of her scarf. Okay, he understood the scarf.

She scratched again. "A rash. I must be allergic to something—or something." She took a tentative sip of her drink. "We decided I shouldn't serve customers today, so I'm leaving early."

He laughed. "Sorry, that's not funny, but now you have a nice fluffy mustache to go with it."

"You do, too." She grinned.

He nearly groaned when she licked her upper lip with her tongue. He'd have loved to help her out with that. He wiped his foam off with a napkin. "So, what plans do you have for your afternoon off?"

"I need to call my mom—another holiday emergency—and finish the plans for the Mayfield Christmas party. Sam and I are the decorating committee." She scooped up a big glob of whipped cream with a spoon.

"Awesome." He watched her lick the spoon clean. "Uh—yeah, that's this Saturday night, right?"

"Yep. We'll start decorating Friday and finish up on Saturday. Hopefully our two high school seniors will be able to handle Friday night and Saturday customers."

"I see The Magic of Chocolate is sponsoring a girls' soccer team this spring. You and Sam do a lot for the community," Joe said.

"We can't wait. The Magic plan to kick Ganon Plumbing and Electric's butt."

"Good luck with that." He sipped the hot chocolate, savoring the rich taste and aroma. "Hmm. I can see why this place is called The Magic."

"Yummy, right? And the name's in keeping with the tourists' interest in all things witchy. I know you don't believe in anything woo-woo, as you put it, but with Salem only a few miles away, why not take advantage and lure in those who do?"

"Sure." He guessed so.

She scratched her neck again. "I'd better get going. I want to get some lotion on this rash before it spreads any more." She gathered her purse and coat.

Joe stood. "Before you go—so, you'll be at the Town Hall party on Saturday. Are you going with anyone?"

"No. I'll be too busy helping out with the buffet line and keeping Sam under control." She wasn't looking at him. He got the message.

"Okay. I'll see you there. I'll be bringing a truckload of toys for the toy drive."

"Super. Thanks for the hot chocolate, Joe." She smiled and hurried out the door before he could grab his jacket and walk with her. He sat back down.

Okay. She was just not interested in him. Wasn't it time he gave up? Not quite yet.

Chapter Two

The next night, Abby sat at a quiet little table in the back of Tres Becheur, the most expensive restaurant in town, happy she was able to wear her slinkiest black dress instead of a turtleneck and pants. Thank all the pickled toads that Sam's salve worked. She was rash free. Her blind date du jour, James, call-me-James, Crabtree, was handsome, rich, the requisite witch, and utterly boring. He'd excused himself to the lobby to take a call on his cell twenty minutes ago. Luckily they hadn't ordered their food yet or she might be eating alone.

Abby sipped her pomegranate martini. Gold was the theme in the large room, thoroughly bedazzled for the holidays. Giant gilded Christmas balls hung from the ceiling on satin ribbons. A tall, noble fir glittering with thousands of twinkling lights and adorned with a forest-full of adorable woodland creatures dominated the entrance.

The large stone fireplace across the room was ablaze. Candles in hurricane lanterns nestled among the pine boughs that decorated the rough-hewn wood mantel. All was rich and elegant and festive. She'd love to decorate the Town Hall for Saturday's party in similar fashion, but they only had the old, tired supplies from the last few years to use. Unless magic—

Wait. What? Joe Ganon?

Yes. Joe sat at a table to one side of the dining room. When she talked to him this morning, she didn't know where she was going on her date and darn him, he never volunteered that he had a date at all. He cleaned up well. He wore a dark sport coat, white collared shirt and navy tie. His long-ish dark hair was neat and tidy. He might have actually used a comb instead of his fingers. Abby could only see the back of his date's head. She had gorgeous wavy chestnut hair held back by a glittering clip. He was smiling in his loopy way and handing her a small gift-wrapped box. Jewelry-sized.

On second thought, her hair wasn't that great and the barrette probably plastic. Abby narrowed her eyes. Miss Mystery Date was too short for him. Or she slumped in her chair. A sharp ache lodged in Abby's chest. The green-eyed monster had her in a choke hold.

Get a grip, girl. Joe is just a friend, remember?

Someone walked into her line of sight. *Oh, Crabtree.* She'd almost forgotten about her own date.

"Sorry, Abby," he said, sitting down across from her. "A fantastic deal…"

Damn. She had to scoot her chair over to look past his shoulder to Joe's table. The woman was unwrapping her gift. Probably smiling sweetly at him. Batting her eyelashes, if she had any.

"…so, I'm probably going to invest."

What? "Oh, yes." Abby was ashamed of herself. She was never this inconsiderate. She pulled her attention back to her date. Crabtree had come highly recommended by her brother. He really did look handsome, all done up tight in his expensive black suit and power red tie. Some kind of gel slicked his hair back. Her brother called him a metrosexual, whatever that was. He was checking out his phone.

"Sounds great, Jim, er James," she muttered.

The waiter came and the next few minutes passed in a flurry of food selections, wine pairings and terrible French accents. She had no idea what she ended up ordering. Something with coq in it. Sam would have snorted.

"So Abby, you said you manage a shop in town?" He snapped his snowy white napkin and placed it on his lap. "A candy store?"

Had he looked down his sharp nose at her? He tried not to be obvious as he glanced at his phone. Again.

"A chocolate shop. We carry homemade as well as imported chocolates and serve coffees and hot chocolate with homemade pastries. We have a fabulous pastry chef."

Over James' shoulder, Joe was standing and so was his date. They were leaving. Wait. No. They were threading their way to her table. Abby dipped her head.

James was talking again, making his point with his hands. Something about the advisability of a college education or else you'll work retail for the rest of your life. Did she just hear right? Abby was formulating an impressive comeback when he placed a hand on her arm.

"Abby, I wondered if you'd go with me to the Mayfield Christmas Party on Saturday."

She swallowed hard.

"How's the rash today, Abigail?" said a familiar voice from above.

James snatched his hand from her arm like she was toxic. Abby looked way up into Joe's hazel eyes, widened in fake innocence. *Abigail my ass.*

"Fine. All better." She offered her bare neck for him to see. He probably had a great view from his lofty height of her fine boobs in this cleavage-loving dress. "Oh, Joe Ganon, meet James Crabtree."

The men shook hands. From behind Joe, a petite woman—no—a girl stepped out. *Holy mugwort and rue.* She couldn't be more than twelve. Joe's date wasn't a date at all. The girl's gorgeous wavy hair swung forward as she offered Abby her hand. In the other, she held the jewelry box. She wore a lovely velvety green, full-skirted dress with a matching shorty cape. She had a sweet, pixy face and a genuine smile.

Abby took a deep breath and exhaled. The monster lifted off her shoulders but left claw marks.

"Hi. I'm Crystal Ganon, Joe's sister." Abby took her hand. "You must be Abby. I've heard so much about you."

"Oh, you have?" *What had that man said?* "Nice to meet you, Crystal." She'd met Joe's two brothers, one older and one younger, when he needed them for a job in town. His other two sisters were pretty, from photos she'd seen. The Ganons were a beautiful family, if not totally dysfunctional according to Joe. She could relate.

Joe introduced his sister to James. "I brought Crystal to Tres Becheur for her birthday. She turns fourteen tomorrow."

"Happy birthday," Abby and James said in unison.

"Thank you," said Crystal.

"We'd better get going. It's starting to snow." Joe took Crystal's elbow. "See you later, Abby."

Abby touched his sleeve. She looked earnestly into his eyes. "Oh, I'll be ready by five on Saturday." She turned to James. "Sorry, James. I didn't get a chance to answer you. Joe had already asked me to go to the party."

"By, uh, five. O-kay." Joe grinned like he just won the best hand at poker. "It was nice meeting you, Jim."

After they left, Abby sat for the next hour and a half, picking at her overpriced coq-au-whatever, listening to James talk about his dry-cleaning empire. She watched him text and wondered how she now had a date with Joe Ganon. Surely, Joe knew she'd only said that to get out of going with James. She could have given him the same excuses she'd given Joe. Could she tell Joe there would be no date with him? Did she even want to tell him? If that thrilling little zing of her nerve endings was any indication, no, she didn't want to cancel.

But holy bat whiskers, time was running out. Only six more days till Christmas Eve and only one more date lined up. Jason Albus had better be love at first sight or Abby was doomed.

In the garage, Joe placed the last of his cleaned-up tools in the aluminum toolbox mounted in his truck bed and closed the lid. Everything was ready for his next job in the morning. The hum of an engine, a rattle and a wheeze told him Abby had pulled her old Toyota into her carport next door. Six-thirty. She was home early from the date she told him about this morning at The Magic. As far as he knew, she never brought anyone home with her. Good. Better than good. Unless she'd gone to their place. Then…

A draft of cold air spun through the open garage door. The soft snow falling outside reminded him he needed to shovel both their driveways. The white stuff had been coming down for the two days since her date with that crab guy, who'd looked a little too, uh, well-groomed. Crab had been a washout while he'd scored an actual date. Maybe not an actual one. That remained to be seen. At least, she hadn't cancelled. Yet. Okay, it was mean of him to ask about her rash. But all was fair in hard-fought love and war games.

God, Abby looked dynamite in that dress. That dipping cleavage was the most he'd seen of her creamy breasts, which made him want to see the rest of her. Naked.

Now he was uncomfortable in his jeans, and cold. When snowflakes swirled in on the breeze, he pressed the garage door clicker. As the door descended he heard a squeak. A body came hurtling through the opening and the door reversed. *Abby.*

"Whew. Just made it," she said, slipping in the wetness. She was bundled up in a warm coat, red woolen scarf and matching hat.

He grasped her arm to keep her upright. It was as if she'd appeared straight from his thoughts. But something was off. No smile today.

"What's this?" In one hand she held a brown box with pink stripes.

"I just delivered one of these to Mrs. Wilson across the street. This one is for you—a Death-by-Chocolate Double-Dare Éclair."

"Thanks. I think." He took the box from her, unsure of what message she was sending him.

"Mrs. Wilson was depressed because her family went home today to Denver. Nothing like chocolate to boost the happiness quotient."

He only needed her, but she looked like she needed a dose of her own medicine. Frown lines creased her forehead. No sparkly eyes. He set the box on his worktable.

"So, how did your date go today?" He assumed the worst. He shouldn't feel good about that but he did.

"Not much to tell."

"This guy is some kind of big-shot entrepreneur, you told me."

"Some kind, yeah. Turns out Jason's a clown who rents himself out for kids' parties."

"That's—not so bad, is it?" Probably not much money in that line of work, but she wasn't looking for a sugar daddy. He couldn't hide his smirk.

"It would be really funny if he hadn't branched out to bachelorette parties and the odd stint at the local strip club."

"A male clown stripper. Thanks for the picture I'll never get out of my head."

"That's not all. He brought his clown suit along just in case I wanted a private lap dance later."

Joe burst out laughing and so did Abby. They finally got themselves under control when a bunch of kids of indeterminate gender, bundled up to their eyeballs, shuffled by on the sidewalk, laughing and kicking up snow. They pulled sleds, hunks of cardboard and round aluminum saucers.

"Hey, Mr. Ganon! Come with us to the hill. The snow is perfect."

He thought the kid might be a boy from his summer league baseball team. He waved. "Maybe I will." The hill was at the dead end of their street. The slope had a tailbone crushing bump on the left and a bunny slope on the right.

He took Abby's arm as he walked her to the sidewalk. She wore fancy leather boots that were definitely not snow grade. Go figure. They stopped under the pale yellow glow from the streetlight. Snowflakes slow-danced through the circle of light, landing on Abby's lashes and red knitted hat. Somehow, she'd stuffed all her hair up under it. He focused on her soft, pink mouth, turned down in a frown.

"Well, I'd better get in," she said. "Endora hasn't been fed yet. You know how she is. She'll be clawing up my leg."

"Hey, I have a great idea that'll cheer you right up."

"I'm not—"

"Come sledding with me. To the hill. I can hear the kids laughing from here. I want to be a kid again."

He saw the thoughts warring in her head, words with long pointy swords. The battle could go either way. She let out a breath that frosted the air.

"Okay." She smiled. "I'll feed Endora and change my boots."

"Good idea. Meet you out here in five."

He sprinted into his garage, his heart doing crazy loops in his chest. *Calm down.* They weren't about to have sex. Not with forty pounds of heavy clothes between them. He grabbed his down parka and gloves from the house, then back to the garage to take down the large silver saucers. *Wait.* What was he thinking? He hung one of them back. They'd share a saucer.

He waited for her under the streetlight, transferring the large saucer back and forth from one hand to the other. The snow had all but stopped. His and Abby's Christmas light displays, which he managed to string a few weeks ago, blinked sequentially, starting at his place and ending around the side of hers. The whole street of restored Craftsmans came together this year with showy, festive displays.

He was about to give up when she opened her door. "I'm coming. Couldn't find my gloves."

She joined him on the sidewalk, bundled up like those kids, effectively wiping out any indication that she was female. He held onto the image of her creamy white cleavage in the sexy black dress. They walked down the middle of the street, bumping shoulders and sliding in the slushy ruts.

"So, do we have a date Saturday, or was I an excuse to get rid of Crabapple?" Joe had to ask.

"Tree. Crabtree. And yes." Abby blew out a visible breath. "I mean, yes to the date. Actually, yes to both."

"I'll help you with the buffet line, but you're on your own restraining Sam."

She laughed. "That would be too much to ask."

When they reached the hill they kept to the right for the easier slope while the kids screamed and laughed their way down the butt bruiser side. Lights from a nearby soccer field illuminated the slopes. He set the saucer on the fresh fallen snow. Sitting down, he scooted to the back rim.

"Come on," he said, opening his legs and patting the small space in front of him. "Fun awaits."

Hmm. Okay, fun might be had between Joe's legs. Yeah, for sure. But...

She looked way down the slope. The bottom seemed a mile away. She carefully sat while he held one of her arms to guide her down on the saucer. Only a partial of each cheek actually made contact. The rest of her wiggled and snuggled into his body. He moaned.

"Oh, am I hurting you?" She tried to twist around to see his face.

"Uh, no. Just stop, uh, wiggling."

"Okay."

"Hang onto the handles and I'll hang onto you. Lift your feet up."

She grabbed the rope handles while Joe pushed off, wrapping both his arms around her. They flew down the slope. Abby screamed just for fun as the wind rushed past, grabbing at her hat and scarf. At the bottom, her feet came down and dug into the snow. The saucer went one way. They went another. She found herself on top of him.

Abby laughed. "Can we do that again?"

Joe wrapped his arms around her. "Sure. I may never be able to father children, but it'll be worth it."

His arms tightened. His hazel eyes warmed, like he'd mixed more cocoa in with the peppermint. A snowflake landed on his adorably crooked nose, broken years ago by one of his crazy sibs. Abby's bones melted into his teddy bear snuggle-ness. She studied his well-shaped mouth, lips full and open slightly, and on how his breath visibly mingled with hers. She wasn't cold. In fact, a hot coal seeped from her midsection and traveled south. She should pull free before one of them did something stupid. Joe was just a friend. A very good friend. Was she still leading him on when she promised she'd stop? She would hate herself in the morning if she let him kiss her.

Abby leaned in and kissed him. His lips tasted like iced caramel double-espresso macchiato. He placed his hand at the back of her head to pull her in deeper and slipped his tongue in to spar with hers. Her racing pulse sounded loud in her ears. She really wished there weren't multi layers of fabric between them. She'd bet her mother's best magic wand and her sister's Sorcerer's stone that his bare-naked body against hers would feel—magical.

Joe pulled back. His eyes searched hers. A crooked smile tilted the corner of his mouth. "We'd better get up or get a room. The kids…"

The laughter and whoops of the children drifted down the hill. "Guess so." She moved off him. The empty cold replaced his amazing warmth. He stood and helped her up. She brushed the snow off the back of his jacket.

Holy toad warts. What had she done? Again? Didn't think, that's for sure. Her self-loathing began as a buzzing in her brain. She hated to wipe that so-pleased smile off his face. "Joe, I—"

A bunch of boys suddenly surrounded them, chattering about how perfect the snow was, try the other side, get airborne, calling them wimps. She laughed at their dizzying enthusiasm. She learned most of them were on Joe's baseball team. She had no chance to talk to him because the kids accompanied them to the walkway near the soccer parking lot that led back up to the street.

They parted ways at Joe's place. He pantomimed "call you later" over the boys' heads and went inside. What she had to say to him couldn't be done over the phone. She must give up their friendship. Abby had no choice. She'd let Joe get too attached. She couldn't seem to control herself around him. There was no way they could remain even platonic friends. Anything more was doomed by the curse to heartbreak for both of them. She'd keep things cool then talk to him Saturday night after the party.

Only four more days till Christmas Eve. Thoughts of what was to come brought a piercing ache to her heart.

Chapter Three

Abby and Sam left the shop on a busy Friday evening in the capable hands of two trusted seniors from the local high school and spent the last couple of hours decorating the large hall. They started with the tall tree at the entrance. It hung heavy with handmade Santas and elves and popcorn balls, donated Christmas bells and tinsel and paper chains. Thanks to Sam the tree was real. The pine's sweetly pungent fragrance reached Abby from across the room.

"This garland looks just plain sad." Sam held up a length of fake evergreen. "I think it's molting, too." She brushed some faux needles off the sleeve of her royal blue sweater.

"I agree," said Abby. "The rest of the decorations are just as tired. They did their duty years ago."

She headed up the too-short stepladder. "Hand that dead creature up to me and I'll try to drape it around the top of the window."

"Hello, ladies."

Joe. Abby cringed. She had avoided him all day after talking to him briefly on the phone. She made sure he left for work this morning before she did. When he came in for coffee at ten, she had hidden in the storeroom. She was such a coward.

"Joe! So good to see you and your great big—ladder." Sam practically tripped over her own feet getting to his side.

Oh, why wasn't Joe interested in her vivacious friend? He handed Sam a small toolbox, but he directed his heart-stopping smile at Abby.

"Hi, Joe," Abby said, climbing down off the stepladder. Her pulse stuttered. Joe was yummy today in work jeans and a nubby, snuggle-worthy beige sweater that made his shoulders extra wide. "What do you think so far?" She swept her arm around the room and swore to herself she would absolutely stop thinking about him in swoony adjectives.

He lugged his extension ladder over to her side. "Well." He surveyed the room. "The real tree's a nice touch."

Sam snorted. "My idea. That fake one had to go. I think something made a nest in the branches and then its many progeny had digestive issues."

Joe laughed. "Good call. So, what do you have left? I remember they had tinsel or streamers hanging from the ceiling last year."

Abby directed the remainder of the decorating while she appreciated Joe and his fine body climbing up and down the ladder. At nine-thirty Joe got a call from his sister Crystal. Some kind of life-threatening situation at his parents' house having to do with a mouse. Joe didn't elaborate, but Abby could relate only too well. All the ladder work was done anyway, so he took off.

An hour later, Abby called it quits. "That's the last of it except for what we'll put on the tables tomorrow."

Sam let out a breath. "Great job, girlfriend." She lifted her hand in a high five. Their hands whooshed by each other without connecting.

"I'm done. Feels a little like home, only less stressful." Abby sat on a long table set up by the entrance and took a sip from a water bottle. "If I were home, I'd be doing the decorating, the shopping, the dinner planning and anything else they say they can't handle." She checked her phone. "See? I have two new messages. From Mom: 'Should I use the gold chargers or the red ones?' From Kaitlyn: 'I can't decide what to get Dad. Help!'"

"You're good at it. You let them take advantage of that." Sam hopped up beside her.

"Pfft. From the look of this room, I just failed miserably."

Sam swung her legs, rocking the table. "We did the best we could with what we had."

"I really wanted to make this special for the town tomorrow night, and the children on Sunday when they hand out the toys. You should have seen Tres Becheur. So elegant, so classy." Abby sighed.

"Well, we could sparkle this place up a bit."

"You don't mean…"

"Attention, Mormon Tabernacle Choir." Sam snapped her fingers. "Deck the Halls" blasted from the sound system. Lengths of red satin ribbon tied themselves in pretty bows on each wreath they'd hung between the tall windows.

"Tinsel bright and bulbs alight," Abby said, pointing her finger at each exhausted garland. They burst into glittering, healthy life. "Fa-la-la-la-la-la-la-la-la."

Shimmering Christmas balls hung from the ceiling ribbons. The tree received an extra heaping of sparkle among the handmades and a thousand more lights. The dozens of donated poinsettias now sat in gaily-painted pots. Abby gauged their magical handiwork. "We'd better dial back the lumens just a smidge. Everyone will need sunglasses tomorrow night." She waved a hand, deducting a third of the radiance without affecting the festive air.

If only she felt that same holiday cheer. The deadline may as well be here, she thought. With only three days left, there was no way she could find someone and fall in love. Even "Jingle Bells" didn't lift her spirits as the enormous weight of the curse lay on her shoulders like a shawl made of chainmail.

—◆—

Joe pulled into the parking space beside Abby's car. Ten-thirty. Sam's car was still here, too. He turned off the engine. The hall lights blazed through the closed blinds. Happy music pulsed from inside. "Deck the Halls"? Appropriate.

He took a moment to unwind after spending the last anxiety-inducing hour trying to rescue Crystal's mouse, Sukie, from the jaws of Clay's giant Maine coon, Hermie. Crystal said Joe was a plumber, after all. When his efforts at reasoning with the thirty-pound feline failed, Crystal burst into tears. She began flinging amateurish magical spells from her fingertips until the house was in chaos. Finally, Joe was forced to resort to magic himself. When the blue haze dissipated, a tiny, soggy Sukie sat on Crystal's shoulder and began her re-beautifying routine.

Why his sibs insisted on accepting their familiars was beyond him. He'd denied the calico cat that frequented his shop and more recently his house, recognizing the creature for what he was. He had been just fine all these years without a familiar dogging his steps.

Magic's power was an insidious siren call luring you to abandon your values, abandon your honor and your dignity. He'd been there, done that, and paid the price with a guilty conscience ever since. Maybe he took the craft way too seriously, or maybe it was just his family's abuse of magic, but even saving his sister from a freak out didn't make him feel any better about using his powers.

Talk about serious, he needed to chill and join Abby and Sam inside. They were having way too much fun without him. He hopped out of the truck and entered the hall's small lobby that reverberated with the sounds of a choir. When he reached the double-door entry to the main room, the music suddenly quieted to a less ear-hemorrhaging volume. He stopped.

Abby and Sam sat with their backs to him on a long table just inside the entrance. He looked beyond them to take in the room and its decorations. He blinked. *Wait. The wreaths. The tree.* He blinked again. Abby was talking. Something about needing sunglasses. She waved her hand. The megawatt glitter dimmed. A string of lights unwound from the tree, dangled in the air and disappeared along with several strands of tinsel.

Joe's stomach clenched into a tight ball. *Abby is a witch.*

He closed his eyes as he let the idea seep into his brain that his normal, sweet, beautiful (had he mentioned normal?) Abby was a witch. She had used her magic to give the old decorations a whopping upgrade. She was talking again. "I don't know, Sam. I'm just depressed, I guess. I haven't found anyone. It's Christmas."

"We tried. You dated a lot of guys."

"One of them might have worked out if I'd given them a chance. I wasted a lot of time with Joe. Every time I turned around he was there and…"

He didn't hear anything else for the roaring in his ears. Heat spread from his chest to his neck. Numbness settled in his limbs, but he somehow managed to about-face and go back to his truck. He sat behind the wheel for a few minutes as he processed how his world had suddenly done a one-eighty into the toilet. Abby was a witch. He'd been wasting her valuable time. He didn't measure up to all those other guys. She wasn't even considering giving him a chance.

Joe started the engine. Could he deal with her being a witch? Maybe. He could deal with anger and frustration. Heartbreak not so much. Heartbreak meant agonizing loss and excruciating pain. How could he feel the loss of someone he never really had in the first place? That kiss. Yesterday on the slopes when she kissed him, he knew she felt something much more than friendship for him. He knew they'd be together forever.

He slapped the steering wheel. Showed how stupid he was. How he didn't know Abby at all. Before that kiss she'd made it clear she just wanted to be friends. He let one kiss cancel out six months of brush-offs. But the thought that he was really just an annoyance, now that crushed him.

I wasted a lot of time with Joe.

He threw the truck in gear, spinning the tires on the icy road. He'd go home and do what men had done since the dawn of dark brews and miserable rejections. He'd swamp his sorrow with a six-pack, punch the wall, and then try to figure out how he would live without Abigail Goodbody.

Abby stuck a large spoon in the center of Mrs. Johnson's Marshmallow Fluff Dream. She set the giant bowl down on the buffet table beside the array of pastries from The Magic. There was enough sugar in the Dream alone to hyper-fuel a daycare full of kidlets for a week. Folks had been arriving at the hall for the last half-hour, some dropping off their potluck offerings, all bringing toys for the toy drive and saying the hall had never looked better. The four-piece combo from the local high school was setting up on the raised platform at one end of the room. Meantime, a DJ played fun holiday CDs through the sound system.

Abby checked the large clock on the far wall for the tenth time. Six-thirty and no Joe. In fact, she hadn't been able to get him all day. He didn't answer her texts or her phone messages. He must have had an emergency call because he was already gone when she got up this morning. She dreaded the after-party when she would have to tell him they couldn't be friends any longer. There was no good way to gently deliver that message. Her stomach knotted.

"Joe's still a no-show?" Sam set a one-ton Costco apple pie down beside the fluff.

Abby figured the town wouldn't come down from their sugar high until next summer. "No, and I haven't heard from him."

"Strange, considering he'd give his right testicle for a date with you."

"He could be caught up in another life or death family crisis or didn't survive the one from last night." Abby knew from experience the difficulty in getting your family to let go. They held on like the tentacles of an insecure octopus.

Then she saw him. He walked in with his brother, Caleb, both loaded down with toys. They headed straight for the corner designated for the donations. He still wore his work clothes of jeans, t-shirt and company jacket as if he'd just stepped off a plumbing job. Abby looked down at her sapphire blue, long-sleeved party dress with the lacy trim and figured one of them didn't get the memo. He didn't smile or look around for her like he always did. Jittery little midges fluttered and nipped at her insides. She hurried over to him as he reached the exit.

"Joe, hang on. You're leaving?"

"Oh, hi, Abby," he said, in an off-hand tone. He nodded at Caleb, who continued out through the doors. "We just brought in a bunch of toys."

"And then you're, uh, staying?"

"No."

Still no smile, or any hint of warmth in his hazel eyes. "What's wrong? Did I—"

"Sorry, but I need to hurry. Caleb is helping me with an emergency job tonight."

"Well, after you're done?"

"I'll be too tired. I've been working non-stop all day." Joe glanced around the room. "Nice job. Looks great."

"Thanks. I guess I'll see you another time, then."

He looked down at her. His dark hair was rumply like he'd pushed his hand through it a few times. She wanted to smooth the silky strands back, smooth out his furrowed brow. She shouldn't be having these thoughts. The critters in her stomach stomped on her nerve endings.

He sighed and broke eye contact. "It's okay, Abby. I wouldn't want to waste any more of your time." He turned and walked out the door.

Waste? Where did he get that...

A knife-edge of pain sliced into her chest. Her conversation with Sam last night. Had Joe come back? How much had he heard? She closed her eyes. The sounds of laughter and the crazy grandma-reindeer song receded into the background. Then her hand flew to her mouth. How much had he seen?

Spirits-of-wizards-and-warlocks. A white-hot blaze raced from her midsection throughout her body, warming her cheeks. Abby's knees went weak. She had to talk to Sam. Her friend's lustrous red organza gown was hard to miss. Abby found her at the buffet table piling sliced honey ham on top of a mountain of scalloped potatoes.

Abby took her aside. "Sam, we've got a disaster," she whispered.

"We will have if you don't let me get back in line. The candied carrots are almost gone."

"Hocus-pocus." Abby invoked their secret code for a magic reveal in front of an Ordinary.

Sam's plate wobbled in her hand. "No." Her eyes grew wide. "No, Abby."

"Yes—well, possibly."

Sam hurried over to the nearest table and set her plate down. She grabbed Abby's arm, propelling her out the door into the small lobby. Thankfully, it was empty.

"Spill," Sam said.

Abby took several deep breaths to calm her pounding heart. Keeping her voice low, she said, "I just talked to Joe."

"He came after all?"

"He just dropped off his toys and left. He said—" Abby's voice shook. "I asked if we could get together after the party, after he was done with some kind of emergency job tonight. I—he—"

Sam made the get-on-with-it rolling motion with her arm.

"He said no, he didn't want to waste my time." Abby had never understood the wringing of hands she read in novels, but here she was clasping and unclasping them.

Sam said nothing for a moment. Abby could see her connecting the dots in that hyperactive mind of hers.

"Oh-my-god! He heard us. He was at the hall."

Not trusting her voice, Abby nodded.

"But how much did he hear, and see?"

"I—I don't know. He only said, you know, wasting my time, in a serious voice I'd never heard before, and then he walked out the door."

Sam paced the short hallway. She peeked in the door where the happy party sounds continued as if the world hadn't come to an end. "Okay. Let's think. We were sitting at the table. Our backs were to the door. Dumb."

Abby nodded. "With the music, we wouldn't have heard anybody come in."

"Then you dimmed the spectacle a bit." She grabbed Abby's hand. "Don't you think if he'd seen actual magic, he'd be, I don't know, a little more freaked out? Like, he'd be home with the doors locked and calling his therapist?"

"He did say, in a calm, rational voice, that the decorations looked great." His lack of expression during the whole, short scene was imprinted on her brain.

"Okay. I'm going to assume he didn't see any magic. Otherwise, no way could he go about normal stuff afterward, like plunging toilets." Sam dropped Abby's hand. She twirled around, spreading her flouncy dress wide like a ballerina's tutu. "I declare our secret safe."

"I guess so," Abby said.

"So, last night you said Joe was wasting your time. Then what?"

Abby pictured them sitting side by side on the table. "Then I said, like, Joe was always around. But I also talked about how much I liked his company, looked forward to seeing him."

"Right. And you said your loser dates couldn't compare to him."

"And you mentioned the word love," Abby said.

"You said you thought so, but that you'd have to end your friendship because of the curse." Sam's mouth turned down. She bit her bottom lip. "I'm assuming he only heard he was wasting your time. He probably left right after." She took Abby's hand again. "Sorry, Abbs. This is a tough one. The only thing to do is talk to him."

Abby's breath hitched. The knife plunged deeper in her chest. Hadn't she decided to end their friendship anyway because any further relationship would result in greater heartbreak? Well, they both were heartbroken now.

"No, I don't think I'll talk to him. How can I explain that yes, he was wasting my time but only because I could have used that time to find my one true love. Sorry, Joe, you don't fit the criteria of the curse that an evil sorceress put on me." Abby's eyes welled. "I need to let this, whatever he and I have between us, die a horrible death."

Sam hugged her. "I'm sorry I couldn't break the curse."

"There you two are."

Abby and Sam jumped.

Mrs. Philpot, third-grade teacher and a member of Choco-holics Anonymous, stuck her nose out the door. "Come on. They're starting the conga line. Woohoo!"

"She fell off the wagon," Sam whispered. "She just spent $100 at the shop."

Abby tried to smile. She was proud that she kept a fake happy in place throughout the rest of the night. She stayed until two a.m. for cleanup and then fell into bed. Tomorrow, oh wait, today, was Christmas Eve. She'd be blessedly busy till into the evening. Less time to think and to bawl her eyes out.

Chapter Four

Joe entered his house through the garage carrying an armload of gifts. Another crazy day spent with family. He wanted to leave right after dinner, but here it was eleven already. Christmas Eve always brought out the extra wacko in his sibs and was the one night he actually enjoyed using magic. They were a competitive, game-playing bunch, but Joe hadn't been in the mood for fun. Being the party pooper he was, he'd upped his amps and won most of them. Well, his powers hadn't rusted with lack of use.

He dumped the parcels under the tiny Charlie Brown Christmas tree that gave off a pine scent despite its straggly branches. Abby had insisted he get a tree, so last week he bought one of the last ones on the lot.

Abby. She'd looked so incredible last night. That blue dress and her huge, blue eyes. Bewitching. He almost smiled at the literal truth. My god, she was a witch. Didn't matter if he could live with that fact or not. She was lost to him. Funny how thoughts became physical blows right to the gut.

Joe hung his jacket in the closet. The house felt cold. He turned on the gas fireplace with the remote for an immediate blaze. He loved this remodeled Craftsman and bought the place the minute he'd seen it three years ago. The open concept space with the bright, modern kitchen suited him. Original wood floors, crown molding and beveled, leaded glass windows helped retain some of the historical charm.

What he needed was a stiff drink. He took a tumbler from the cupboard by the sink, splashed in a little Jack. Damn. The faucet still dripped. He'd get to it tomorrow. Or next week. He glanced out the window. Abby must have just come home from her day with family. Every light in the house was on. She hated dark corners.

He carried his drink to the easy chair by the fire and sank into the soft cushions. He'd brood a little and feel real sorry for himself for a while. Maybe a few days. Years. And then what? He didn't have an answer. He still wanted her. Badly.

As soon as Abby came through her door, Endora raced over and meowed. She scooped the cat up in her arms, burying her face in the pure white fluff. An affinity to the thoughts of animals, especially familiars who could read you right back, had been handed down through her family for generations on her mother's side. Endora knew all about Grimm and the curse.

"I know, my sweet. It's almost midnight and I'm just exhausted, but I'll get you food." Her family had been especially needy this Christmas Eve. She'd ended up helping with almost every aspect of the day's activities, sometimes resorting to magic to get everything done.

She'd turned down the offer to spend the night but found the forty-mile drive home in the dark through skiffs of snow stressful. She set her familiar down. With a wave of her hand her coat flew to a hook by the door. Another wave turned on all the lights in the house. Glass Christmas balls that Endora had stolen from the tree littered the living room floor. None were broken thanks to the large colorful area rug.

"Back to the tree, one, two, three." The ornaments returned to their branches.

Endora followed her into the kitchen and leaped up on the counter. Abby called for the bag of Kitty Kibbles kept in the pantry as she retrieved the cat dish from the floor.

"Meow."

"I know. I'm hurrying."

Endora jumped to the windowsill over the sink. "Meow."

"What?" Over Endora's head, Abby saw that Joe's lights were on. "Yes, he's home. So?"

"Mee-oow."

"Dingbats and Sabbat bells, Endy." Abby poured the cat food and set the dish down on the floor. Endora stayed where she was. Abby heaved a huge sigh. The ache in her heart had followed her for days. The pain grew stronger as the midnight deadline approached. She wished she had Sam to talk to instead of her familiar, but Sam was probably all snuggled in bed with Dave receiving his Christmas gift. Sam's words.

"I know I should apologize to Joe. I killed him this time. But how do I explain?"

The first time she'd rejected him was like a skin-deep poke of the knife. They'd only known each other for a couple of months when she gave him the let's-just-be-friends speech. But ever since she did nothing to discourage him from falling in love with her except refuse to go on an actual date. Oh, she knew he was in love with her. He was just biding his time until she gave up on finding someone else. Then she kissed him in the snow. Of all the insanely dense, thoughtless, crazy wonderful...

Friday night she'd thrust the knife to the hilt when he overheard part of her waste-my-time conversation.

With the cat at her heels, Abby went into her bedroom to change. She opened her dresser drawer to pull out PJs. Endora jumped in the drawer, turning in circles on top of her pretty night things. She meowed like the lovesick calico tom that had hung around outside. Kind of like Joe, poor guy.

"Let me get my pajamas. I'm not going over there now. It's after eleven-thirty."

The cat rolled onto her back in typical ragdoll fashion. The blue-eyed breed had a lot of adorable idiosyncrasies, but Abby was not amused. Not this time. She sat on the edge of her bed.

"I want to remain friends with him, Endy, but can two people just be friends when they're so attracted to each other?" Abby knew the answer even if Endora didn't. No, not usually. Or never. She sighed. "All right. The least I can do is try to explain what I was saying to Sam and hope that he forgives me." She ruffled the fur on Endora's head. "I sure hope I don't regret this. I would hate to have to move."

She glanced at the bedside clock. Eleven-forty-five. Hopefully he'd agree to let her in. She'd be with him when the deadline came and went instead of all alone having a pity party with a cat. Perversely, she set the alarm on her phone to chime the dreaded hour and stuck it in her jeans pocket. She went back out to the kitchen followed by Endora. Gathering together a few wrapped chocolate samples from the shop, she put them in a pretty Magic bag along with the gift-wrapped Boston Red Sox coffee mug she'd gotten him for Christmas. He was a die-hard fan and, well, she didn't want her gift to be too personal.

"Wish me luck, Endy."

Abby put her coat and boots back on and headed next door with her parcel. As soon as she stepped off her porch, the crisp, frigid air frosted her nose. Her eyes watered. All down the street, Christmas lights twinkled merrily. They were trying desperately to cheer her up. Were Joe's lights, perfectly synchronized with hers, a sign they were meant to be together, if not as lovers, then as friends? Wow. Talk about reaching for fanciful straws.

Except for her soft footsteps, the silence was utter and deep as the snow piled alongside the road. Joe had swept his porch clean. There, lying on the porch swing as if he owned the place, was the calico tom. He blinked his bright green eyes. Joe didn't have a cat. He was more of a dog person. A weird thought popped into Abby's head. From the cat? Joe was—special?

"What—"

The door opened. Abby jumped. "Oh, Joe." He had on his jacket. "Are you going out?" His hair had the bed-head look, all sticking up on one side. There were lines under his eyes she'd never seen before. He'd probably been working himself to death. But there was a spark in his eyes, a determination in them that she had seen before. His mouth, at first set in a firm line, drew up in a smile. Every taut nerve in Abby's body began to relax.

"I was just coming to see you," he said.

"You were? I—I have a gift for you. A Christmas gift. It's small. Well, not tiny, but—I mean, it's not very much—"

His mouth came down on hers and his arms went round her. Thoughts flew everywhere in her brain. What did this mean? Did he already forgive her? He tasted deliciously like whiskey and pumpkin pie. This was heaven.

When he finally pulled back, she was breathless. "Oh, wow. I—I thought you must hate me for what you overheard." He shook his head, a quirky smile tilting his mouth. "Sam and I figured out you must have overheard us talking in the hall." She squeezed his shoulders. "If you'd stayed long enough, you'd have heard that I, well, love you. I love you with all my heart."

She closed her eyes. Oh, by the spirit of Biddy Early, why had she blurted those fateful words? Was she dooming them? She opened her eyes again.

Joe ran a hand through his hair, which didn't improve on his bed-head. His smile turned into a happy grin. "I never thought I'd hear you say that. You know how I feel about you, Abby. I think it was love at first sight." He set her away and held both her hands. She no longer felt the cold. In fact, he'd added a few logs to her internal furnace.

"This is going to sound really arrogant, but here goes. While I was sitting in there with my glass of Jack, I figured out the only reason why you've been resisting me."

She laughed. "Believe me, it was hard."

"You were looking for someone—special. Really special."

"Wait—" The cat still lounged on the swing. It licked one paw and swiped over an ear. Abby's head buzzed. *Special.*

Joe took in a deep breath and let it out. "You're a witch, and I'm the witch you've been looking for."

Abby clutched at his hands to keep from falling. "You're a witch? How? I mean you don't have the faery mark."

"Oh, I do. It's lower on my body than most. My sister Reese and I are the only ones in the family with the mark out of place."

"On your beautiful, hard—okay." She set the bag on the porch floor. "Kiss me again. Quick."

And he did. A deep, all consuming, body-on-fire kiss. She stood on tiptoe and threw her arms around him, opening her mouth to allow his tongue to play with hers. Her chest seemed to expand and her blood to surge through her veins. Her old tormented heart pulsed with new life as if it shed its mossy cover. A lightness of soul enveloped her. She believed she could float away on its euphoria.

Her cell phone chimed in her pocket. She pulled away from him to shut off the alarm. "Midnight." The word came out on a breathless sigh. Every nerve cell in her body buzzed with sweet energy. A joyous rapture bubbled up from her insides.

The curse is lifted. The damn curse is lifted!

"Um, does something turn into a pumpkin?" Joe glanced around the porch.

She laughed. "Let's go inside and I'll explain."

She grabbed the bag from the floor as he opened the door for her. Something brushed against her legs. A furry blur of black and orange dashed in ahead of her.

"That cat is your familiar, you know," she said. The animal jumped up on Joe's favorite chair by the fire, circled once and lay down. Abby put Joe's gift with a pile of others under his adorable Charlie Brown tree.

"I know." He hung up their coats, stopping on the way back to stroke the cat's head. "Damn cat. I didn't want a familiar. Guess I got one anyway." He came and took her in his arms. "I'm glad you're here."

Abby felt his smile and his happiness clear down to her toes. His eyes shone, not with triumph, although he'd won a mighty battle, but with absolute love. "Me, too. Let's sit. I need to explain."

He sat beside her on the sofa and took one of her hands in his. "Can't wait to hear this one."

She covered his hand with hers. "Let me start by saying a lot of stress, heartache and bad dates could have been avoided if we could sense other witches."

"I can sense the most powerful ones like my uncle. But I didn't have a clue about you until I saw your magic at the hall."

"And I can sense Hilda Grimm. She's the powerful sorceress who put a curse on me. She commanded that I must fall in love heart, soul and mind with another witch by midnight tonight, or I'd never find true love. All of my romantic relationships would end in heartbreak." Abby squeezed his hand. "I never wanted to put you through that." She explained why Hilda had cursed her.

"I should have my uncle pay Grimm a little visit," Joe said through clenched teeth.

"This crazy ordeal is all over now." She patted his arm. "What I can't quite figure is why the curse wasn't lifted Friday night when I told Sam I thought I loved you."

"Hmm. Let me see. Didn't you say Grimm said you must fall in love in 'heart, soul and mind'?"

"Yes."

"Maybe you weren't accepting the possibility in your mind because you thought I was an Ordinary."

"That's it! Yes, I love you with my heart and soul, but my stupid brain had to play catch up."

"Just in time, apparently."

Abby hated to think what would have happened if she'd waited a few more minutes to come over. Thanks to Endora, she hadn't. "How about a drink to celebrate true love and the lifting of the curse?"

Joe started to get up, but she pulled him down. "Hey, dude, don't go anywhere. We have the magic." She waved her hand. His once-empty glass on the coffee table in front of them now held a splash along with a glass for her on the rocks.

"To tell you the truth, I don't do magic on a regular basis," he said.

"Oh, you're one of those." She kissed him on his crooked nose when he arched his brow. "But I won't hold it against you."

He laughed and gathered her in his lap. "My family exploits their magical powers all the time. Makes me crazy when they call me to fix their screw ups."

"I know what you mean. You have a family of eight and I have a family of six—all helpless."

"Deal breaker?"

She snuggled into his warmth with a contented sigh. "No way. But really," she said. "I only use my powers in emergencies or when I'm exhausted, or like now, when I'm way too comfy to get up."

He snapped his fingers. The glass appeared in his hand. "Yeah, too comfy."

"So, about your faery mark," she said.

Joe waggled his eyebrows. "I'll show you mine if you show me yours."

And not too much later they did just that.

Barb DeLong writes the magic of love and laughter and happily ever after.

Barb DeLong has always had a passion for reading and writing. She has won and been a finalist in several writing contests. Animals are another passion, and creatures both wild and domestic are featured in most of her stories of love, laughter and magic.

Barb contributed contemporary romance stories in *Romancing the Pages* and *Secrets of Moonlight Cove* anthologies. The *Love for Christmas* anthology includes her paranormal short story *A Witch for Christmas*. She's working on a humorous paranormal romance series called *Charmed by a Witch*.

A transplant from Canada, she enjoys the sunny climes of Southern California with her one-and-forever hubby and a fluffy, blue-eyed ragdoll cat, two children and five grandchildren.

jill jaynes
aug 20, 2021

The Christmas Wish

by Jill Jaynes

"You're not behind the couch, you're not in any of the empty boxes, and you're definitely not under the bed." Allie dropped the edge of the linen bed skirt back down and pushed up from her hands and knees. She leaned her elbow along the top of the mattress. "Where is that cat?"

This was the worst part about moving—getting her cat adjusted to a new home. Phoebe didn't like change, and moving back home to Southern California from Chicago was a lot of change for one little gray tabby.

"Cheer up," she called to the empty room, and hopefully her cat. "This is the last move you'll ever make, Phoebe. We're both home for good now."

Standing up, she tugged the hem of her black sweater dress down her thighs. "I'm definitely not dressed for cat-hunting. At least if I don't find you I won't need to roller cat hair off of me before my date gets here." She headed back down the hall to the living room, the heels of her boots *thunking* firmly on the solid oak floor.

Make that *her* living room. Her very own signed, sealed and mortgaged living room right here in Southern California. Back home where she belonged, close to the family she'd missed so much more than she'd expected to when she'd first decided to accept a music studies scholarship from the University of Chicago.

She was only a ten-minute drive from her parents' house now, a huge improvement over the six-hour flight away she'd been for the last six years.

Her hard work and sacrifice had paid off when, much to her practical parents' surprise, her Ph.D. in Musicology landed her a position as a music professor at a private university right back here in sunny Southern California. She was home for good now, ready and eager to start her new life.

She couldn't help pinching herself just a little as she soaked in the Christmas warmth of her decorated living room. One whole corner was taken up with the bushy, 7-foot fir tree she had splurged on—a far cry from the sad little table-top trees she'd settled for as a lonely, struggling student.

The Christmas tree had always been the centerpiece of the holiday during her growing up, and decorating it wasn't complete until her mother's little porcelain shepherdess had been hung in the place of honor at the front of the tree. Allie had purchased all new ornaments this year for the first real tree she could hang them on, but somehow it still seemed incomplete without that one, special ornament.

Well, she was just making a start, she told herself. This was only her first Christmas here, the first of many more to come. This year, she would have her parents near her and hopefully in the not-too-distant future she'd have her own little family to start new traditions with as well as enjoy the old ones.

Through her living-room picture window, she eyed the twinkling lights that newly decorated her neighbor's house across the street. *Hmm, somebody must finally be home.* The place had been uninhabited as far as she could tell since she'd moved in two weeks ago. Nobody came or went, but the interior lights came on every night, clearly on a timer.

She was glad to see the decorations, but they highlighted the fact that hers was now the only house on her side of the street without them. Maybe tomorrow she'd borrow her dad's ladder and gather the courage to climb it and hang some lights of her own.

But first things first. And first right now was to locate her kitty before her date got here. She'd rather not leave the house not knowing where Phoebe was, but if she didn't find her in the next twenty minutes, she wouldn't have much choice.

As she worked her way through the living room one more time—bending to peer under the couch and loveseat, checking behind the curtains—she kept an ear tuned for her date's arrival. Never know, he could show up early.

She had a good feeling about this one.

His MatchUp profile showed him to be a nice-enough looking guy in his early thirties with brown hair, a warm smile and a mischievous glint in his eyes. He'd recently moved to Newport Beach from Chicago to take a job as an executive for a popular chain of home improvement stores (his new model BMW seemed to back up his story) and best of all, claimed to be looking for his "last first date." His pictures showed him to be up for the kind of wholesome fun her heart yearned to share with someone special—horseback riding, playing Frisbee at the beach and smooching with his brother's Irish Setter dog.

If Tim Warren had been truthful on his MatchUp profile, and was as easy to talk to in person as he'd been in the two phone conversations they'd had, he could be the total package.

She hadn't had much luck in the last few years with the guys she'd met online, or with the guys she'd met offline, either. But then, the dating pool at the University had its limitations. Guys online were either looking for a quick hook-up, or were not in her league, to tell the truth. In school, the motivated, goal-oriented guys she was attracted to were too busy chasing those goals to think about dating. That pretty much left only the aimless "professional students" who weren't worth wasting a perfectly good evening on. She'd finally realized that although she might be lonely for a connection with someone, she hadn't been in a position herself to get into a relationship, and had reluctantly given up trying to meet anyone.

But this time was going to be different. She could feel it. Because now she knew what she wanted and was ready to meet the kind of man she was looking for. Someone who knew who he was, was ready to establish himself, and start building a life.

The doorbell chimed. She pressed her hand to her stomach where butterflies began their frantic fluttering and stepped to the door. *This can't possibly be Tim*, she admonished herself, and pulled it open to find her parents standing on the stoop.

"Hi, sweetheart!" Her mom pressed a quick kiss to her cheek and swept past her into the house, trailing her signature cloud of Chanel.

"Hi Mom," Allie said to her mother's back. She turned to greet her father. "Hi Daddy, good to see you." She wrapped her arms around his waist for a real hug.

"You too, pumpkin." He leaned down and dropped a kiss on the top of her head.

She smiled up at him at his use of the familiar nickname. "I'm nearly twenty-seven and I'm never going to grow out of that name, am I?"

"Not as long as I'm around, you're not. You're the only daughter I've got, so I guess you'll just have to live with it."

"Works for me," she said. Releasing him, she pulled him into the house. "Come in already, it's cold out there."

Her father snorted as he followed her into the living room. "You've only been back in Southern California for three months, and sixty-four degrees is already cold to you? Those Chicago winters should have toughened you up. How's your heater working, by the way? Everything okay?"

Allie grinned. "My heater is fine, daddy. I'm fine. Guess you can take the girl out of California but you can't take the California out of the girl."

Her dad slung his arm around her for a quick hug. "Have I mentioned how glad I am you're back home again? Right where I can keep an eye on you." His grin was teasing, but Allie heard the note of seriousness underneath it.

Allie laughed. "I think you may have mentioned that once or twice when you called earlier to check on the whether the automatic sprinklers had come on this morning." She glanced up at him. "You know I can take care of myself now, right? I mean, I appreciate all your help, but I survived clear across the country for six years all by my little self."

"I know, I know. I'm just an over-protective dad, and you'll always be my daughter, no matter how old you get. I don't think I'll be changing anytime soon."

Taking a slow circuit around the living room, Allie's mom was dressed to kill in a little black dress accented with just the right amount of sparkle. It was tastefully short, and combined with her four-inch heels, showed off her legs nicely. She wore her short blond hair in a sleek cut, exposing her Christmas bulb earrings.

"Wow, Mom. You look great." She glanced at her father, in his pressed slacks and black suitcoat. "You look pretty spiffy yourself, Dad." He might be a little past the big five-O, but his blond good looks were holding up well. "I'd forgotten how nicely you clean up."

He grinned. "All your mother's doing, I assure you. I just put on what she lays out on the bed. You're looking beautiful as always. Although maybe those pretty blond curls are a little too nice for a night in front of the television. Got plans?"

She leaned a little closer to her dad and lowered her voice. She didn't want to get her mother started on one of her famous cross-examinations. "Got a hot date, actually. He'll be here in about fifteen minutes."

"Ah," said her father, laying a finger along one side of his nose. "Your secret's safe with me."

She loved her dad.

"Allie, you've done an amazing job with this place." Her mother paused in her stroll to run a finger along the arm of the shabby-chic wingback chair where it kept the overstuffed sofa company in front of the fireplace. "Very vintage-cottage, which works perfectly in this little house. I've always loved wood floors and white walls."

Allie warmed at the praise. Her mother was an interior decorator by profession, after all. "Thanks. Me too. I know this style isn't the sort of thing you usually go for, but I like it."

"Well that's what matters, isn't it?" her mother said with a smile. "After all, this is your home. Which brings me to why we stopped by."

"I was wondering about that. I'm assuming you didn't get all dressed up just to come see me."

"Much as we love you, you're right. We only have a minute. We're on our way to your father's company Christmas party, but I wanted to make sure and give you a little housewarming gift." She held out a small white box with a red ribbon wrapped around it.

"Wow, thanks Mom." Allie took the box, giving her mom a quick hug around the neck. Pulling off the ribbon, she lifted the lid.

"For your first Christmas in your new home," her mother said, as Allie drew out the Christmas ornament nestled inside.

"Oh, Mom." Allie swallowed hard against the lump in her throat as she cradled the little porcelain shepherdess in the palm of her hand. "Are you sure?"

"This ornament has been handed down from mother to daughter in my family for five generations," her mother said. She closed Allie's fingers around the figurine. "It's yours now."

Allie smiled at her mother and blinked back the tears that pricked behind her eyes. "Thanks. Thank you so much." Allie pressed a kiss to her mother's cheek. "I'll take good care of her."

Her father cleared his throat. "Yes, well. We'd better get a move on, Elaine." He glanced at his watch. "Parking can be a challenge at this place."

"Of course, Ken," said Allie's mother. "Why don't you go start up the car and I'll be right out."

"I guess I know what that means." Allie's father gave Allie another quick top-of-the-head kiss and headed for the door. "Must be some 'girl talk' I don't need to hear," he said with a grin. "Don't take too long."

Elaine waited until the door snicked closed. "There's something else I have to tell you." She stepped closer to Allie and lowered her voice, as if afraid of being overheard. "This ornament is more than just an heirloom. There's magic in it."

Allie widened her eyes. "Who are you and what have you done with my practical, 'there's no such thing as the Tooth Fairy' mother?"

Her mother smiled. "I'm telling you what my mother told me and her mother told her. It's part of the deal. The ornament is always handed to the oldest daughter on the first Christmas in her own home. And on that first Christmas, you get to make a wish. Just one. And it will come true by Christmas Eve. It has worked for at least the last five generations that I know of."

"Are you telling me you made a wish and it came true?"

"If you ever tell a soul I'll deny it." Her mother glanced past Allie's shoulder out the front window at the car where her husband waited. "But I did. And it did."

"Wow. Well thanks, Mom." Allie looked down at the little porcelain figure in her hand. How had she never known about this?

"Remember, you get just one wish and one chance at it, so make it count—the more specific, the better. Don't waste it on world peace. This is just for you."

She strode to the door. "I'd better get going. Don't want to keep your father waiting too long out in the 'cold.'" She grinned.

"Wait, what did you wish for?" Allie had to know.

Her mother stopped with her hand on the doorknob and turned back. She shrugged a shoulder. "What else? True love. Bye now." And with a last swirl of perfume, she was gone.

Allie gazed at the figurine in her hand with new eyes. She couldn't have asked for a better present. If her serious, no-nonsense mother actually believed the ornament had been making wishes come true for the last five generations, there must be something to it.

She knew one way to find out. And she planned to be *very* specific.

She stood in front of her Christmas tree and curled her fingers around the ornament. How did one make a wish? There ought to be a formal way to do it.

"Here goes nothing." She closed her eyes. "Star light, Star bright." The childish rhyme came to her lips unbidden. "I wish on this ornament here tonight." Yeah, that sounded about right. "I wish I may, I wish I might, have the wish I wish this night." She wrapped her fingers tighter. "May my true love come to me tonight."

The glass seemed to warm in her palm, and a low buzz hummed through her, but it could have been the furnace vibrating in the walls.

She opened her eyes. Nothing looked different. She didn't feel any different. But then, she didn't know how these things were supposed to work. She was willing to have a little faith.

A bubble of happiness and possibility rose in her chest. Her date was about to arrive, the most promising candidate she'd met in a long time, and she may very well have just locked in the deal.

Now, if she could only find her cat in the next five minutes.

"Mrrroooowwww." Phoebe's misery cry was muffled but unmistakable. It seemed to come from the kitchen.

"Oh my gosh. Where *are* you, cat?" Allie rushed to the kitchen and began opening each of the lower cabinets in a methodical frenzy. She'd already searched this favorite hiding place, but Phoebe could be moving around.

Beep! Beep!

She stopped her search to peek out of the kitchen window. A low-slung sports car waited in front of her house, the lights on and the engine running. *He's here!* She put her hand to her stomach—the butterflies had grown to an entire flock. She could see the driver sitting behind the wheel, but couldn't make out any details in the dim light.

Beeeep!

"Am I late?" She glanced at her Felix the Cat clock above the sink. Seven-thirty on the dot. Clearly, he was a punctual person.

Hurrying to the living room, she scooped up her leather jacket from the back of the couch. She grabbed the doorknob, but then bit her lip in indecision. Damn! What was she going to do about her cat?

Maybe she could ask Tim to wait a few minutes while she wrapped this up.

She pulled open the door, and almost walked right into the man who stood on her front step. He had one hand raised, poised to knock. With the other he held her cat against his chest.

Her very dirty, and decidedly unhappy, cat.

"Phoebe! *Bad* kitty, where have you been and how did you get outside?" she scolded. She looked up at the man standing before her. Way up. From the strong arm that cradled her kitty, up to a handsome face with a firm jaw and nice green eyes.

This definitely wasn't Tim.

At least she thought it was a handsome face. It was a little hard to tell, since, like the cat, he was covered with dirt from head to toe. Like he'd rolled in it, run through a sprinkler and rolled in it again. His hair might be light-colored under all that dirt, but she wouldn't put money on it.

"Hi there. I believe this is yours."

"Um, yes." Allie hesitated, not wanting to take the cat from him and end up with the same dirt all over her own clothes. "Why don't you come in for a minute so you can let her loose?" She held the door wider. "The last thing I need is for my cat to make another run for the great outdoors." She sighed inwardly. She supposed a dirty cat in the house was better than a clean one that she couldn't find.

Beep!

The man on her doorstep raised his eyebrows and looked over his shoulder at the Beemer. "That for you?" he asked as he stepped across the threshold.

"Sorry, that's my date," said Allie, peering around her unexpected visitor to wave at the car outside. "I'll be right there," she called, hoping the driver could hear her above the hum of his running engine. She bit her lip and glanced between her dirt-encrusted cat and the car at the curb. She hoped she wasn't messing up her chances before the date even started.

"Let's make this fast," she said, and shut the door. "Okay, you can let her go."

"Sure thing." The man bent and gently released the cat, who made a beeline for the hallway.

Allie couldn't help but sigh as she eyed the muddy footprints the cat left behind. "She's probably heading for my pillow." She'd deal with the dirt trail later. *After* her date.

She turned back to her benefactor. "Thanks so much. I've been looking everywhere for her, but I have to leave and I didn't know what I was going to do."

"No problem." He stood and smiled at her, and something about that smile tickled at the back of her mind. Something familiar. "That's what neighbors are for. I live across the street."

"Oh, right. Neighbors. Well, nice to meet you. My name's Allie." She started to reach out to shake his dirt-encrusted hand, then pulled back.

He laughed, and looked even more familiar. "No, you don't want to touch me. You look way too nice."

"You're really a mess." She knew she'd seen him somewhere. It was in the shape of his mouth and the slight crook of one tooth. "I'm assuming my cat is somehow responsible for all this. Sorry."

"Yeah, she was hiding under my back deck and it took a little digging to get her out. No problem—I'm glad to help. I don't know what I'd do if I lost my dog. He's like my kid or something." He peered at her intently. "I guess you don't remember me."

She narrowed her eyes. "You look familiar, but I can't seem to place you."

"Yeah, it's been a few years, I guess. I'm Matt Young. Your brother's friend?"

Allie gaped. "Brian's friend Matt? Skater-boy Matt?" The last time she'd seen her brother's loser friend Matt, he was slouching his aimless way through junior college. "You've sure grown up." *Had he ever.*

He ran a hand through his hair, and grimaced at the dirt that rained onto his face. "Yeah, well, that's what a few years in the military will do. I was with your brother in Afghanistan, actually. I got out after one tour. He decided to stay and make it two."

"Right," said Allie, still trying to wrap her mind around the fact that the hunky, muscular guy (with definitely blond hair) standing in her entry-way was the same kid who'd hung out with her brother and teased her for studying so hard. "I just got a letter from him the other day. He's supposed to get out in June."

"Yeah. He's a real tough guy. One of the best guys I know, too." Matt shook his head. "Well, I knew you were moving in sometime this month. I would have come over sooner to say hi, but I've been out of town."

She opened her mouth to ask him how he'd known she was moving in when a single, demanding *Beep!* blasted from the car outside. With a last glance around the room to ensure Phoebe wasn't crouched somewhere, waiting to make another break for the great outdoors, she pulled the door open. "Hey, thanks so much for finding my cat, but I've really gotta run." She hustled Matt outside ahead of her, then closed and locked the door behind her. "See you around. Have a great night."

She trotted down her walkway to the waiting car, hoping she hadn't kept her date waiting too long. You only got one chance to make a first impression, after all. When she reached the car, the driver pushed open the passenger side door from where he sat.

"Jump on in," he called to her above the rumble of the engine. "I've got us reservations at a killer restaurant in Dana Point, but we've gotta boogie."

"Oh. Okay." Allie got in, pushing down the unkind thought that he could have taken a minute to get out and open her door from the *outside*, it being their first date and all. "I guess killer restaurant reservations wait for no man," she said as she buckled her seat belt.

She turned to find him looking at her with an appraising smile that melted her doubts. "Wow, cute *and* smart," he said. There was that twinkle. Cute in his pictures, downright irresistible in person. "Did *I* get lucky! Hold onto your seat belt."

With that, he hit the gas, and the car leaped effortlessly to rocket speed. It was all she could do not to scream like a teenager on a roller coaster. She could get used to this!

Hopefully, her special Christmas wish would make sure she hadn't gotten them off on the wrong foot.

Matt rubbed the finishing wax into the last section of the hood of his Mustang convertible. The cherry-red paint glowed back at him, catching the mid-morning rays of another perfect California December day, the kind that made everyone on the East Coast want to move here.

From his driveway, he eyed the little house across the street and wondered again about Allie and her date the night before. He'd watched with a frown as she'd hustled past him to let herself into the high-end sports car. He wasn't too impressed with the guy she was going out with if he couldn't manage to get out and open the car door for his date.

He knew from experience that guys were on their best behavior when they first met a woman and cared about making a good impression. It was all downhill once they got comfortable. If last night was an example of this guy's best behavior, Allie's future with him didn't look all that promising.

He bent again to waxing his car, focusing on coaxing out a perfect, high-gloss sheen.

It wasn't that he was jealous or anything. He was just watching out for his best friend's kid sister, that's all. Like he'd promised Brian, still serving in Afghanistan.

A promise was a promise, especially when it came to Brian. They'd been friends since they were both eleven years old and Matt had been the weird new kid in school for the third time in as many years. Matt had been getting his ass kicked by a group of snotty grade-school bullies who had surrounded him in a quiet park on his way home from school. Again. The next thing he knew, Brian was standing back to back with him, backpack thrown aside, fists up. "Got your back, man," he'd said. They'd had each other's back ever since.

Brian's family had accepted Matt like he belonged there. Their door was always open and there was always an extra seat for him at dinner if he was around. As a kid who got little attention from his often-absent parents, Matt thrived in the safe harbor Brian's family offered him, soaking up their gentle guidance. Over time, Brian's dad had proven more of a father to him than his own father had ever been.

So when Brian sent a letter letting him know that Allie was moving back to California, and asking a favor, of course the answer was yes. "Watch out for Allie," he'd written. "She's a smart girl, but she's not street smart, you know? She's sweet, and people take advantage of her. Especially guys. Keep our girl safe, okay?"

He'd thought this was an easy "yes." But then last night had happened.

Holy crap, it had never occurred to him that the scrawny, shy high-school girl he'd last seen eight or so years ago would have grown into an accomplished, not to mention smoking-hot, woman. The picture of her dressed in that form-fitting black sweater-thing and thigh-high boots the night before played like a movie in his head, seriously messing with his memories, not to mention his best intentions.

"Hi neighbor! How're you doing today?"

He looked up to see Allie crossing the street towards him, all long legs and golden skin in her denim shorts and tank top, a foil-covered plate in one hand. *Merry Christmas to me*, he thought, silently thanking the weather gods for the unseasonal, superheated Santa Ana winds as he watched her approach.

She stopped at the end of his driveway and gave a low whistle. "Nice car." She offered him the plate. "Here, these are just a little thank-you for rescuing my cat yesterday. I did some baking yesterday."

He took the plate and lifted the edge of the foil. "Christmas cookies. Awesome." Snagging one with frosting and sprinkles, he popped it into his mouth. "Mmmmm," he groaned, closing his eyes as buttery flakiness melted in his mouth. "These are really good." He grabbed another one and took a bite. "If you were hoping I'd be polite and offer you one, you're out of luck," he said around a mouthful of cookie. "My manners just aren't that good when it comes to sharing homemade goodies."

She laughed, and he found he couldn't look away from the cute way her nose wrinkled. *Whoa, watch it, buddy.* He didn't have to wonder at all about what Brian would think about Matt lusting after his little sister. This girl is off limits.

She tilted her head and gazed at him. "You look like you're doing well for yourself, Matt."

"I do okay." He smiled back at her. "I have your dad to thank for kicking my butt and getting me into an Electrician certification program. I actually worked on your house remodel."

"Wow, I didn't know that. Thanks!" She smiled at him, doing that cute nose-wrinkle thing again. "I'm impressed." Interest danced in her sky-blue eyes. "Sounds like you're way overqualified to do the favor I was going to ask you for."

He glanced down at the plate in his hand and gave an exaggerated sigh. "I knew there'd have to be a catch." He grinned at her so she'd know he was only teasing. He would do just about anything for her. *For his best friend's little sister, that is.* "These are pretty damn good, though, ain't gonna lie. Ask away."

She laughed. "I'll have to remember that for next time."

Matt's heart skipped a beat. There was already a next time in his future. Nice.

"Sooo, Mr. Electrician, how are you at hanging up Christmas lights?"

"As it happens, I'm quite the expert, but I don't come cheap." He scratched his chin. "How many more cookies have you got? Maybe we can work something out."

"Oh, great! That would be wonderful!" She clapped and bounced up and down. Her smile lit up her whole face, and she was just so damn cute and perky with her pretty blond ponytail. Matt was entranced.

"You're easy to please, aren't you," he kidded.

"This means a lot to me. It's my first Christmas in my own place and I just want everything to be perfect. There's no way I can do this myself." She leaned closer, and gave him an excellent view straight down scoop neck of her top. He licked his lips and tried his best not to stare. At least not too obviously.

Her lips curved, and the amused look she gave him told him she knew exactly what he'd been staring at. She didn't seem offended, so that was good. "I don't even have a ladder yet," she confided. "And to tell the truth, I'm a little afraid of heights."

He didn't even care that he'd been outed. Just because he hadn't turned down an opportunity to look down a hot girl's top didn't mean he didn't respect her, or that he wasn't going to look out for her. *Right, that's why you're defending yourself,* the little voice in his head laughed.

He told the voice to shut up, and looked Allie right in the eye. "Got you covered, Allie. Did you want me to do it today?"

She bit her lip. "Would tomorrow be okay? I'm heading out for the beach in a few minutes, soon as my date gets here. But I should be home all day tomorrow."

Matt kicked his disappointment to the curb. Of course she was going out on a date. She was smart, beautiful, and single. She probably had hordes of guys running after her. He should be thinking about her like she was his own little sister, maybe offering advice instead of ogling her.

Too late, bro, the voice in his head said knowingly. *Nobody checks out their sister's rack.*

He'd get his head straight. Somehow. "Tomorrow's fine. Ten o'clock work for you?"

"Perfect," she said, just as a silver BMW Z4 with the top down roared to a stop in front of her house. The horn blared.

Why was he not surprised?

"Oh! There's my ride. I'm outta here. See you tomorrow at ten." Allie turned and jogged across the street to the waiting car.

Matt eyed the driver, who was currently waving at Allie with a big canary-eating grin. As irritating as that was, he couldn't really blame the guy. He'd probably be wearing the same grin if Allie were jogging over to *his* car.

The guy had short, dark thinning hair, high-end Ray-Ban sunglasses that screamed money and an entitled attitude. But overall, Matt supposed he looked pretty conservative. Maybe he could be a safe choice for Allie.

But the fact that he couldn't get out of that car and open the door for her nagged at him. As Allie bounced around the front of the car to the passenger side, the smile turned into something much more predatory and assessing.

Too bad money can't buy character. Matt's fists curled with the urge to knock the leering look off the man's face.

As soon as she folded herself into the passenger seat and closed the car door, the driver peeled away from the curb in a showy display of horsepower.

"Get some manners, dude," Matt called after the car as the brake lights flashed and it disappeared from sight around a corner.

He was definitely going to have a talk with Allie about demanding better treatment from the men she dated.

* * *

Allie leaned her head back against the headrest of the low-slung convertible, the steady purr of the engine rumbling through the plush leather seat. She wished she had one of those gauzy white scarves to wrap around her neck so the ends could flutter behind her as they drove.

She couldn't help but notice the envious looks other drivers cast their way as they cruised down the highway towards Newport Beach. She would be envious, too, if she were looking on from the outside. She was with a great guy in a hot car, heading for the beach on a postcard-perfect Southern California day.

A nice-looking, smart, successful, single guy who was, from all appearances, kind of into her.

Everything was going so great, she felt like pinching herself to make sure she wasn't dreaming. They'd had a great time at dinner the night before, talking and laughing, swapping stories about Chicago winters and childhood Christmases. Tim had suggested they take the long way back, then headed up Pacific Coast Highway, hugging the coastline while the moon shone like a floodlight on the ocean. She'd reveled in the warm, salt-laden night air—so much better than shivering while walking home on icy sidewalks.

After a quick drive-by of his *very* nice neighborhood in Newport, he'd taken her home, ending the evening with a sweet goodnight kiss and plans to meet in the morning. He'd texted her good night before she'd made it into bed. It seemed like the ornament's magic was working, because it was by far the best first date she'd ever been on. She couldn't wait to see how the second one would turn out.

An hour later found her wiping sweat out of her eyes while she dog-gedly pedaled her beach-cruiser bike against a stiff ocean breeze. What had she been thinking, agreeing to a marathon bike ride up the coast when she hadn't even been on a bike in five years?

Up ahead on his own bike, Tim turned his head to shout something back at her. Not that she could hear him. Not now or the other dozen times he'd done the same thing. He was apparently in much better shape than she was, because he'd kept about a twenty-foot lead on her since they'd left the bike-rental place and it didn't seem possible to catch up to him.

When he'd originally suggested renting cruiser bikes and riding along the beach, Allie had jumped at the idea. The beachside boardwalk was full of people gliding effortlessly on their balloon tires, dressed in shorts, biki-nis and sunglasses. She couldn't wait to join them. And Tim had been so excited, insisting they use his phone to take pictures of each other on their bicycles in various poses before they started out.

Turned out, it was more work than it looked.

Allie peered at the seemingly endless stretch of unbroken bike trail ahead of her, and searched for a glimpse of the Huntington Beach pier they were supposedly heading for. She really should have thought this through. She was getting tired a lot faster than she'd expected, and they'd still have to ride all the way back to where they'd started. All those nights *not* going to the gym after work were paying her back now, that was for sure.

Unable to hear anything Tim said, Allie shouted into the wind towards him. "Maybe we should get some lunch somewhere soon."

Miracle of miracles, he slowed down and waited for her to catch up. "I think we should get some lunch," he said. "There's a place up here that makes great sandwiches."

Allie smiled, hoping she didn't look as exhausted as she felt. "Sounds great!"

To her relief, things got better after she got some food in her. Leaving their bikes locked in the stands at the sandwich place, they strolled along the sand towards the waves.

He slung an arm around her waist as they walked, and Allie leaned into the feeling of closeness. Maybe there really was something to this Christmas wish business.

He checked a lot of things on her list, after all. He had a great career that he'd been working at for a while. He was settling down here in Orange County, and he was looking for a relationship, not just a good time. He was about the right age, at his thirty-four to her twenty-seven, and although Allie couldn't help but compare his average five-foot-eight build to Matt's six foot-something muscular frame and broad shoulders (which, she had to admit, had been set off nicely by his simple white t-shirt this morning), he was better looking in person than he'd been in his photos on his profile. That dangerous little twinkle in his eyes, highlighted by good-natured crinkles at their corners, made his smile infectious.

Tim was a great conversationalist. He clearly liked talking about himself, but he asked her a lot of questions as well and seemed genuinely interested in the answers. He also had an endless store of amusing stories about other women he'd met online through MatchUp.

He took hold of her hand and pulled her towards the water. "C'mon, let's get our feet wet. You'll feel better."

As her feet hit the firm, wet sand near the water, she breathed in the salt of the air and let the mist of seafoam tickle her nose. Ah, this was one of the things she'd missed the most about living in California. *Sorry Lake Michigan, you just can't compete with the Pacific Ocean.*

Tim headed straight for the water, keeping a firm grip on her hand. Allie pulled back on his arm. "I wasn't planning on swimming."

Tim only picked up the pace. "Who said anything about swimming?" Water splashed up and out from her feet she jogged to keep up with him through the shallow slide of water that sped over the sand. Still Tim ran on, and soon she was knee deep in churning water that pulled at her, gathering its force to head back out to sea.

He released his hold on her, only to turn with a wicked gleam in his eye. "Water fight!" he yelled and scooped water at her in big arcs with both hands.

"Tim! Stop! That's not funny." Allie instinctively held her hands up, but of course it was useless against the sprays of water that soon soaked her shorts and white tank top. "I told you I didn't want to get all wet." She tried to rub the salt water out of her eyes, which of course only made them sting worse.

"C'mon, Allie, loosen up," he laughed. "It's only water, you won't melt." He closed the distance between them, taking her in his arms in a too-tight embrace. "Besides, we can always go back to my place. My hot tub will warm you right up." He lowered his voice to murmur in her ear. "It's totally private. You won't even need a bathing suit."

"This isn't funny." She pushed at him, trying to break his hold. "And I'm not getting into anybody's hot tub." She didn't like the way he was rubbing his body against hers. Her wet, clinging clothes made her feel somehow naked and exposed where she pressed against him.

"In fact," she said, angling to get her hands against his chest in a way that would break his hold, "I want to go home. NOW."

"Fine," he said, and released her—at the exact moment she pushed with all her strength. She landed hard on her bottom just as a wave rushed at them, washing over her head and tumbling her in the powerful surf.

She coughed and spluttered as the water retreated, wiping at her eyes as she sat up. *Now I know what a washed-up piece of seaweed feels like*, she thought. *I probably look like one, too.*

"Allie, oh my God. I'm so sorry. Are you okay?"

She looked up to find Tim reaching out to take her arm, shock written on his face.

"I've been better," she said, accepting his hand. She stood with as much dignity as she could muster.

"Tell me what I can do to make this up to you. Just name it."

The remorse on his face went a fair way to making her feel better. He clearly hadn't meant anything nefarious by his actions. He just pushed a joke too far, that's all.

"I'll think of something." She sighed, and looked down at her soggy clothes. *Oh well*, she thought. *It's only water.* Her brother had done worse to her when they were kids.

But the fun had gone out of the day for her. She crossed her arms against the goosebumps the wind raised on her wet skin. "Right now, I really just want to go home." She turned and marched back up the beach towards their bikes.

Tim rushed after her, almost dancing in his haste to make amends. "Sure, of course. Whatever you want." He acted like he wanted to take her hand, but she kept her arms crossed and her gaze straight ahead as she goose-stepped through the thick sand.

She swerved to miss a couple sitting on a towel, kissing, completely oblivious to the world around them. The guy was tall and lanky, and the way the fabric of his shirt stretched across his shoulders made her think of Matt. *Bet Matt wouldn't push you into the water*, a little voice in the back of her head pointed out. *Bet he's a really good kisser, too.*

Wait, what? Where had that come from? She wasn't interested in her brother's friend Matt. Even though she'd thought he was kind of cute in a skater-boy, rebel way when they were both teenagers, she'd never looked back once she took off for college. *Seems like he turned out pretty okay, though, huh?* Her little voice jabbed at her.

Allie shook her head. She already had Mr. Right on the line. She didn't need to be thinking about other guys right now.

When they reached the side of the snack shack where they had left their bikes, Tim stopped her.

"Tell you what," he said. "I'll ride back and get the car, then drive back and get you."

Allie sighed. "I wish I could take you up on that." She bent to wipe the sand off the bottoms of her feet. She'd always hated wearing shoes with sand in them. "But there's nowhere to put a bike on, or in, your car. It doesn't even have a backseat."

Tim scratched his head. "Oh yeah. You're right. Sorry. At least we won't be riding into the wind on the way back. Maybe you'll warm up?"

"Sure. Maybe." She wheeled her bike around to face back the way they'd come, hiding her smile. He really did look miserable. Enough that she was pretty sure he was working on ways to make up for this little episode.

She got onto her bike and started pedaling, Tim right beside her this time, talking to her, trying to make her laugh.

Things were going to turn out fine, she thought, as the hot sun dried her clothes faster than she'd have thought possible. There was no point in fighting the magic in a Christmas wish, now was there?

———◆———

"Phoebe, I swear, if you don't move you're going to be wearing tooth-paste." Allie clamped her toothbrush between her teeth and shoved her inquisitive cat away from the bathroom sink faucet. She leaned down to spit, rinsed several more times and bared her teeth at the mirror. Good enough. She had to get a move on if she was going to be ready when Tim arrived in fifteen minutes.

He'd been really sweet yesterday during the drive back to her house after the semi-disastrous beach date, ending with an offer to pick her up for a drive to Malibu the next morning. "No bikes," he'd promised, hand over his heart.

She stepped back into her bedroom and pulled on the halter-style sundress she'd laid out on the bed. Lightweight and a little clingy, the turquoise fabric set off her hair and eyes and a few other things, too. It would be perfect for a beach day. The bedside clock read nine-fifty. She'd be ready at ten, no problem.

Ten o'clock! She slapped her forehead. Matt was going to be here at ten to start hanging Christmas lights. She'd been so tired last night from her bike ride and full of the next day's plans that she'd completely forgotten about canceling with him. She'd taken a bubble bath and curled up on the couch with Phoebe and a bowl of popcorn to watch a hapless Sandra Bullock in *While You Were Sleeping,* one of her favorite Christmas movies. She'd fallen asleep somewhere in the middle of it—leaving Sandra to work out her own problems, waking much later to rolling credits. Yawning, she'd shuffled off to bed to finish what she'd started.

It all crashed into her now, though. She'd better get over there and let him know so she didn't keep Tim waiting when he got here. She grabbed her phone and headed for the front door. She had her hand on the knob when her cellphone buzzed.

She frowned down at Tim's number on the screen, then punched to accept the call. "Hi there," she said. "On your way?"

"Hey, sorry, but I'm gonna have to ask for a rain-check. My dad came into town last night and my brother and I are taking him to brunch this morning."

"Oh, okay. Sure." Allie knew she sounded like a disappointed little kid, and made an effort to rally. "Have a good time with your dad."

"Will do. I'll make it up to you. Promise. Call you later."

"Bye," she said, as the disconnect signal beeped.

A loud clang from the backyard got her attention. Cellphone in hand, she rushed to the sliding French doors that led out to her small backyard. *Looks empty to me,* she thought as she reached for the door handle. Maybe the noise had come from next door.

She pulled open the slider, just glimpsing the gray streak at her feet that was Phoebe tearing out the door a split second too late to stop her.

"Phoebe, come back!"

Great. She was pretty sure her cat didn't know where home was well enough to reliably return to it. Heaven only knew where she would hide this time.

"Phoebe," she called, stepping out onto her nice new redwood deck. The Santa Ana winds were still in force, making it summer outside. Would've been a perfect day to go to Malibu. Instead she got to hunt for her cat. Again.

Grape ivy spilled from the planters built along the tops of the railing. As she laid her cellphone on the glass-topped table, she made a mental note to get some poinsettias to put out here. Not real ones—they were poisonous to animals. But silk ones would do.

Striding out onto the grass, she turned the corner at the back of the house and ran face first into the metal rungs of an upright ladder.

"Ow! What the—" Tears sprang to her eyes at the blow. Her hands flew to her face. Her ears rang.

"Allie! Are you okay?"

Strong hands gripped her shoulders. She couldn't quite get her eyes to focus on the face peering down at her, but she could see through her fingers well enough to tell it was Matt.

He frowned. "Maybe you should sit down."

"I'm fine, I think." She tried to push away, but only managed to stumble forward. Against a big, warm wall of chest.

His arms instantly came around her, and it felt so good, so right, that for a moment she let herself lean against him and enjoy being held up. Or maybe just being held.

"Whoa, what's your hurry? Just breathe for a minute."

Her ears were still ringing and she couldn't actually seem to trust her knees to hold her up at the moment, so, fine. Maybe she *would* just rest here with her face on his soft gray t-shirt and breathe for a minute.

She closed her eyes and inhaled. The scent of Matt's warm skin and whatever laundry soap he used filled her nose. His heart thumped steady and calm beneath her ear. She hoped she wasn't bleeding on his clean shirt.

"What are you doing here, anyway?" she grumbled into his chest.

"Getting a head start on putting up your Christmas lights. This'll be the coolest part of the day and I had some extra sets I thought I'd use. Hope they're okay. I've already got the front of the house done."

"Oh. Sure. Well, thanks. I think." She stepped back, supposing she'd stayed in the secure circle of his arms for about as long as could be considered neighborly. She was surprised by the feeling of loss that stung her, even though he kept his hands on her shoulders to steady her.

"Let's see how bad this is."

Matt inspected her face, his expression intent. His eyes, in the sunlight, were a striking moss green fringed with short curling lashes. This close, she could see the single hairs of his day's growth of beard on his cheeks, light gold in the sun. She wondered if they would feel soft or rough against her own skin. Soft, she'd bet. They looked soft.

Whoa, back it down. What was she doing thinking about Matt's facial hair?

The way he winced as he brushed her hair back from her face told her what she already suspected.

"Yeah, you've got a good bump coming up," he said. "I'm really sorry. I just wanted to surprise you."

Allie touched the swelling with careful fingers. "You definitely surprised me. I'll be wearing the proof on my face for a week." She suddenly remembered Phoebe. "You didn't happen to see which way my cat went, did you?"

"Sure, she's right there."

A dog barked close by. It could almost be in her yard. She looked around Matt.

It *was* in her yard. And it had Phoebe.

"Oh, my God!" Allie ducked around Matt and ran toward the animals, where a gray and white dog the size of a lion had her poor helpless kitty on her back by the throat. "Stop him! Help! Somebody stop him!"

"It's fine—" said Matt as he grabbed for her arm from behind. "It's my dog. They've already—"

Allie kept running across the grass, her one thought to pull the dog off of her cat, but pulled up short. Both animals had stopped what they were doing and were staring at her as if wondering what all the commotion was about. Phoebe blinked up at her from her upside down position, while the dog lifted its massive head, tilted it to one side and opened its jaws in a doggy smile.

"—met," Matt finished. "They're friends."

"Wha-a-a-at the heck is going on here?"

Matt stepped up beside her. "That's my dog, Chewy. They spent about three hours together under my deck the other day. Chewy wouldn't come out without her."

Allie stood with her hand over her racing heart, trying to process Matt's words. Then Phoebe took a sucker-punch swipe at the dog's jowls, rolled onto her belly between his paws and began to clean her fur as calmly as if she were on her own fluffy pillow. Chewy nuzzled the top of her head, leaving it wet with slobber.

"Oh." Her voice sounded high-pitched in her ears. Probably from all that extra adrenaline that pumped through her when she thought her cat was being torn to shreds. "Okay. So, we're good here."

Matt took Allie's elbow. "Boy, you've had a hard morning. Maybe you should go inside and relax."

"Yeah. No. I'm fine." She shook off his hand, still not able to quite believe her eyes as her cat got up to take an unconcerned stroll across the grass with the dog snuffling at her heels. "I just never would have guessed my cat was a dog person."

Matt laughed. "He kinda grows on you. C'mere, Chewy." Matt patted his leg and the dog ambled towards them, his long whip of a tail waving high. "He looks a little intimidating, but he's just a big teddy bear."

"He's big all right," said Allie, eyeing the dog as he got closer. She reminded herself there was nothing to be afraid of. If her kitty trusted him, surely she could too. "I haven't been around dogs much. My brother was allergic when we were kids, so we never had one."

To her surprise, Chewy walked past Matt and stopped in front of her. He leaned his full weight against her thighs and looked up at her over his shoulder, tongue lolling in a big ridiculous doggy smile.

She reached out and patted his back. "He *is* nice. Not scary at all."

"Neither of us are." Matt rubbed at the scruff along his jaw line. "We just look that way."

Allie thought the only thing scary about him was how hot he was: all hard muscle, firm jaw and careless spiky blond hair. Then there were those green eyes that seemed to see more than she wanted to show.

As he stepped closer to scratch Chewy's ears, his arm brushed against hers, sending a whole frisson of little tingles along on her suddenly sensitized skin. "He's always trying to rescue somebody. Cats. Baby birds. Little old ladies crossing the street. He scared the heck out of some little kids when he tried to give them back a ball they kicked into the yard."

Allie laughed, more than a little jealous of the caresses he lavished on the dog. "I'll bet. Sounds like the two of you have a lot in common."

"Hey, I don't drool nearly as much as he does."

She grinned. "I mean the rescuing part. First you rescued my cat, now you're putting up Christmas lights."

She couldn't get over how different Matt was from the way she remembered him. He sure wasn't an aimless kid anymore. He was caring and funny and had an air of rock-solid reliability that drew her like a magnet. He'd become a man over the time she'd been away. A man with broad shoulders and a well-toned six-pack she'd gotten up close and personal with a little earlier.

For a second, she wondered about her wish, and whether she was getting it right. She shook it off. *Of course I am. I was thinking of Tim when I made the wish.*

"I'm not really that nice." He offered a lopsided grin. "I was told Christmas cookies were part of this deal." He leaned closer and waggled his eyebrows. "There *are* cookies, aren't there? 'Cuz if there aren't, I'll just pack up my killer ladder right now and be on my way."

Allie held up her hands, palms outward. "Hey now, don't quit on me. There are most definitely cookies. And maybe some iced tea. Or beer or something."

He squinted at the sun. "A beer might very well be in order at some point. Guess I'd better get to work."

Matt forced himself to step away from Allie, when all he could think about was how much he'd like to pull her back into his arms where she'd been a few minutes before. God, she felt good. He slung a coil of Christmas lights over one shoulder, and gripped the ladder where it leaned against the house.

"Step back now." He checked over one shoulder to make sure Allie was clear as he stepped up the rungs. "I wouldn't want the ladder to jump out and smack you in the face again." He set to work, laying out the next length of wire to staple into place.

"Ha-ha. Very funny."

Matt turned to glance down at her and lost his breath for a moment. She stood with her arms crossed and he tried hard not to salivate at the sight of her breasts plumped up in the low "v" of her halter dress, begging to be admired. *And touched. Maybe tasted, even.*

Holy crap, did he need a cold shower or what? This was his best friend's little sister. The girl he'd promised to look after, not lust after.

"Uh, just kidding." He cleared his throat and tried to clear his mind. His mind was having none of it, however. He wasn't going to be un-seeing that spectacular view for a long time and that's all there was to that.

With a stern warning to himself to get back to work and quit ogling the customer, he concentrated on laying a string of lights along the roofline.

"So how was the date yesterday?" *Ka-chunk.* In went another staple. He unwound more lights and shifted his balance to the right a bit.

"It was fine. Why?"

"Just wondering. What'd you guys end up doing?"

"We rented bikes down at the beach. Had lunch and came back. It was… great."

Matt caught the hesitation. Mr. Speed Racer's leering smile flashed through his mind. *What else had happened down at the beach yesterday?* "Bikes, huh? Looked more like you went swimming than bike-riding when you got home yesterday."

"How do you know what I looked like when I got home yesterday? Are you spying on me or something?"

Matt glanced down to find Allie frowning up at him, one fist on her hip. He knew enough about women to read the warning starting to flash in her eyes, but suspicion that she was hiding something dug its spurs into his protective instincts. *If that jerk had done anything to Allie yesterday—forced himself on her, hurt her in any way…*

His blood pounded in his ears at the thought, shocking him with the strength of his reaction. He was beginning to understand why Brian thought she needed looking-out for. Allie was much too nice a girl to be left on her own to swim in the dating shark tank. He set his jaw and dug in his heels.

"Hey, I was out in my garage, minding my own business, when your 'boyfriend' dropped you off and peeled out in front of your house." Matt climbed down the ladder, moved it a few feet over and climbed back up. "Pretty sure he meant for the whole street to notice." Actually, based on the smug look the guy had shot at him, Matt would bet money it'd been meant mostly for him.

"So he's got a nice car. So what?"

So he's a douchebag. "Nothing. My car has a lot of horsepower too, but I don't feel the need to prove it to the world every time I come or go." Something had happened on the date. Something she didn't want to talk about. *Ka-chunk.* Matt pictured the guy's smug face. He pictured knocking the knowing smile right off it. *Ka-chunk. Ka-chunk.* "So, you ride your bikes into the ocean or something?"

"We went to the beach and got wet. Not sure why you need to know."

"Hey, I'm just making conversation."

"No, you're not." Her tone told him she was on full alert now. "You're totally grilling me." She narrowed her eyes at him. "It's my dad, isn't it? Are you spying on me for him or something?"

"Of course not." *It's your brother.* "Nobody is spying on anybody." He cleared his throat. "Unless you count looking out for your best friend's little sister as spying."

"I see." She sounded a little crestfallen. "How *brotherly* of you." It clearly wasn't the answer she'd been expecting. *What answer* had *she been expecting?*

She frowned up at him and crossed her arms again, and the thought of other guys enjoying that view, especially the loser she'd spent the last two days with, sent the last of his good intentions went up in smoke. He might as well admit that his feelings about Allie went a lot deeper than a promise he'd made to her brother.

He gritted his teeth and climbed down the ladder to stand before her. His realization shook him to the core, but he'd have to deal with it later. Right now was about keeping Allie safe.

He had about a half a foot in height on her, so she still had to look up to meet his eye and heaven help him, those luscious breasts were in touching range. "Listen," he growled at her and kept his eyes on her face with an effort. Her very angry face. "I'm just trying to look out for you. Is that so bad?"

She raised her chin, and glared at him in response.

His own temper flared. He was on the high road for once, and he still got crap. *Bring it*, he thought.

She did. "Well, I'm a big girl now and I can look out for myself just fine. I know my Dad still thinks of me as his little girl, but I can't have him checking up on me like I'm a kid, and I don't need you helping him."

She took a step closer and poked a finger in his chest. "The last thing I need is you sticking your nose in my business. So thanks, but no thanks." She turned on her heel and marched across the grass toward the patio.

He stomped after her. "You know what?" he called to her retreating back. "You're right. You're not a little kid anymore. Not by a long shot. But I'm gonna do you a favor and give you some free advice anyway."

She spun around so fast he almost ran right over her. "Oh really," she said.

This close, her scent reached out to him from her warm skin, something part flowery and all Allie. Her cheeks were flushed, her eyes bright, and her breathing was fast. For a moment he imagined she would look just this way aroused by passion instead of anger. He fisted his hands at his sides to keep from pulling her into his arms and kissing her until she forgot she was angry.

For a split second, he thought he saw the same thing flash in her eyes.

"Yes, really," he said, pulling himself back to what he wanted, no needed, to say. "You need to check yourself on the kind of guys you date. Seriously, is Mr. Speed Racer the best you think you can do?"

Allie stepped back and stuck her chin even higher in the air. "I don't need any advice from you about who I date. Tim is a great guy, with a great career who happens to be *very* interested in me. And who I happen to be very interested in, too."

Matt snorted. "Well, I'm here to tell you Allie, that you deserve way better than a guy who honks at you from the curb. He should treat you like a lady, and you should expect him to."

"He treats me just fine," Allie shot back.

"Wow," Matt shook his head. "You really think it's too much to expect him to get out of his car, walk up to your door and knock like a gentleman, for Chrissakes? That would be treating you like a lady. Or maybe if that's too much, he could at least think about opening the car door for you instead of sitting there revving the engine while you run out there at his beck and call. Hell, you're probably apologizing for keeping him waiting while you're at it."

Allie slid her gaze away. "Tim is a very punctual person. It's not his fault I'm not ready when he arrives."

Matt took her by the shoulders. "Listen to me, Allie. You are selling yourself way too short. And I'm not just saying this because you're my best friend's sister and I promised to look out for you."

"Of course you are." Allie glared at him, challenge in her eyes. "That's exactly what you just said you were doing."

Matt stepped closer, hyper aware of his hands on her skin. Her incredibly soft, warm skin. Allie swayed closer to him. It took every ounce of self control he owned not to answer that challenge and prove her wrong. Throw his stupid promise to the wind and show her how much he cared about her. He tried hard to remind himself that she wasn't his girl. She was his best friend's sister.

"No, I'm saying it because I can't stand to see you let some loser guy convince you that you are lucky to have him, when the exact opposite is true." Unable to help himself, he lifted one hand to smoothe a strand of honey blond hair back from her face. "Can't you see you are too good for him, Allie? You are intelligent, successful, and way too hot for your own good."

Allie stepped closer. "Really? And what does that make you?" she whispered.

"A pretty lousy friend," he said, and kissed her.

His mouth came down hard on hers, demanding and devouring and she couldn't get enough. Everything was fire—his touch, his taste, and how much she realized she wanted this. Wanted him. She twined her fingers into his hair and pressed against him as his arms closed around her, locking her close.

From the patio table, her cellphone began to blare the Beach Boys, "Wouldn't it be Nice." Tim's ringtone.

Allie froze.

"Let it ring," Matt murmured against her lips before taking command of her mouth again.

What about your wish? An insistent little voice hammered in her head in rhythm with the Beach Boys as Matt did amazing things with his tongue. *You have to stick with the plan.*

God, how she wanted to tell the voice to take a hike. It didn't feel anything like this with Tim. But the voice had a point. She'd only get one shot at this wish, if her mother was right. She had to give it a fair chance to work.

She forced herself to pull back and release her death-grip on Matt's hair. "I've, um, gotta get that."

Matt dropped his arms and stepped back, looking suddenly embarrassed. "Right. Uh, sorry Allie. Didn't mean to—you know."

Allie turned and ran for the phone, glad for the excuse not to have to explain further.

Somehow seeing Tim's name displayed on the caller ID didn't make her feel any better about the disappointment she'd read in Matt's face as she'd stepped away. "Hi," she said into the phone with a brightness she didn't feel. "How's your dad?"

"Hey, change of plans."

She hadn't realized before how nasal Tim's voice sounded over the phone. Not like Matt's deep tones. "Dad decided to head down to San Diego to see my sister," he continued. "So I'm free. How about a drive down to Dana Point?"

"Um, sure. Yeah." Allie winced. *That sounds convincing.* "I mean, I'd love to."

"See you in about twenty."

"Okay. Bye."

Allie headed back out into the yard and around the end of the house. Matt was up the ladder again, working on the lights. "Hey, there." She shielded her eyes with her hand as she looked up at him. "Um, I'm going to be taking off in a little bit here, but you can stay as long as you need."

"Sure thing, Allie," he said, clearly focused on lining up his next shot with the staple gun. "You do whatever you've got to do. I can take care of this."

She stood there, watching him for a minute, trying to make sense out of her feelings. How could she be so attracted to two men at the same time? No, to be honest, the way she felt with Tim wasn't even on the same attraction-meter as the way she felt with Matt.

Still, there was the wish. Maybe she should just have a little faith and stop trying to second-guess everything.

"Thanks, Matt." She paused. "For everything. It means a lot to me. I'll bring some cookies by later, if that's okay."

"Sure, whatever," he said. He hadn't looked at her once since she'd left to answer the phone. *Ka-chunk.* He uncoiled a couple of loops of lights from his shoulder. "Catch you later."

"Right." Allie turned away and walked back to the patio. She scooped up Phoebe where she lay sunning herself on a patio lounge chair and pulled open the slider to retreat into the house. She stole a glance back at Matt, who was fastening a final string of lights. "Later."

***

Tim was almost an hour late to pick her up for his company Christmas party. An hour that Allie had spent re-prepping her hair, re-rolling cat fur from her little black dress, and re-checking out the front window whenever a car passed in the street outside. Like now.

Nope, no cars. Just Matt's Christmas lights glowing cheerily at her from across the street.

Allie checked the time on her phone again and sighed. Three minutes later than the last time she'd looked.

She wondered what he was doing tonight. They hadn't really talked at all since the day he'd put up her lights. Oh, he was polite and pleasant enough in passing, in a totally neighborly sort of way. But every polite wave came with a sharp little jab of regret. He clearly stayed on his side of some line that had been drawn that day.

Unable to help herself, she rang Tim's number once more, but just like the last two times she'd called, it went straight to voicemail. Maybe his battery was dead.

She shifted in the wingback chair where she'd made herself sit in a concentrated effort to stop pacing and stared at the TV. She'd finally turned it on to get some background noise going so she'd stop jumping at every little sound. One of the many sweet little Hallmark Christmas movies kept up a sociable patter that made her feel slightly less alone.

The lights on her Christmas tree winked at her, and her gaze was drawn, again, to her mother's porcelain shepardess in its place of prominence in the center front of the tree. She was really starting to wonder about this wish-thing.

The last several weeks had been a little… bumpy. The first week or so, Tim had been so interested, insistent on seeing her almost every day. Her determination to give the wish a chance to work had seemed to pay off. But soon he'd become nearly unavailable, cancelling plans more often than he kept them. Usually at the very last minute. When they did manage to get together, everything seemed fine. Still, doubt niggled at the back of her mind.

So she'd been thrilled when he'd invited her to this party. This would be the first time she would meet some of his friends and coworkers. It would also be the first time she would spend the night at his place. It seemed like a step forward in the relationship.

She wondered what was keeping him. She grabbed her laptop from the coffee table and flipped it open. Out of habit she scanned her email, checked out FaceSpace, and with barely a conscious thought, opened up MatchUp. She clicked on Tim's profile—at least she could look at his picture if she couldn't get the real thing—and gasped.

There he was, on a perfect Southern California day, sitting in his two-seater convertible with the top down and the Newport pier in the background. There he was standing beside a beach cruiser bike on the sidewalk in front of the bike rental place, and there he was on the bike, hamming it up for the camera. For her, she'd thought.

After all, she was the one who'd taken the pictures.

But here were those pictures on his MatchUp profile page, and there was only one reason for them to be there.

He was still looking.

Outside, a car horn blasted.

—◆—

"Come away from the door, Chewy, there's nothing out there worth barking at." Matt rubbed a calming hand over the dog's head and split the blinds on the front window to peer outside. He wasn't surprised to see the familiar BMW parked, motor running, in front of Allie's house. "Just the usual douchebag alert."

He dropped his hand and shook his head. Why did it still get to him every time he saw Allie trotting off on another date with that loser? She'd made her decision perfectly clear the day he'd hung her Christmas lights—Tim was the guy.

And Matt was left with the role of friend.

Still, he couldn't seem to break himself of the urge to strangle the guy every time that bozo pulled up and honked in front of Allie's house. And every time he watched her quick-step to the waiting car, he wanted to run out there and shake her.

But he'd had his chance. He'd made his case, and she'd made her choice. He needed to get over it and move on.

Unfortunately, knowing what he needed to do and doing it were two different things. To his dismay, he was having zero success with turning off his feelings for Allie. He'd just known her too long, most of her life really. He knew her folks, where she came from. Allie was really good people. She was sweet, beautiful and smart. Well, maybe not street-smart. She let the wrong people walk all over her.

That's why she needed someone who would treat her the way she deserved to be treated and look out for her when she didn't look out for herself. Someone like him.

He looked out the blinds again. He knew what was going to happen and it made him crazy that there was nothing he could do to stop it. Allie was going to give her heart, and that scum-bag was going to trample all over it. After that, she was going to sit and wonder what *she'd* done wrong.

Across the street, Allie's door opened. But this time, she didn't run out like usual. This time she held her ground.

"If you want to see me," she yelled loud enough that he could hear her over the car idling in the street, "you can come to the door like a gentleman!" She punctuated her declaration with the slam of the door.

Matt went on full alert. Something was about to go down. When emotions ran high, things could get out of hand real fast.

He grabbed Chewy's leash from the hook beside the door and clipped it on. "C'mon, boy. Let's take a walk."

———

The doorbell rang.

Allie stared at the door for a moment, fuming. Too little, too late, she thought and pulled it open.

From the walkway below the porch, Tim looked up from checking his watch. He gave her his most charming lopsided smile. "You ready to go?"

Allie pursed her lips a moment. "You know, I'm really not." She stepped to one side. "Why don't you come in?"

"Sure. Okay. Thanks." He stepped in, and after apparently thinking better of an impulse to try for a kiss, walked past her into the living room.

For a moment, Allie just stared at him. All five-foot-seven, thinning hair and leering grin of him. She'd thought he was cute, and funny. Sexy even, in his own way. Mostly she'd thought he had everything she was looking for: established in his career and his life and looking to share it with one person. Until she'd seen him online three minutes ago—still shopping.

She felt sick. She'd been so stupid.

"I want to show you something," she said and stepped back to the chair where her laptop rested, Tim's profile page still displayed on the screen. She picked it up and turned it around for him to see. "Care to explain this?"

He glanced at the screen, then back at her. He tilted his head. "What?"

She pressed her lips together. Discarded a half-dozen or so replies that came readily to mind. Tapped her foot for the count of five. Still, Tim remained silent, not even trying to explain or excuse what was plain for anyone to see there on his dating profile.

"Wow. You can't even be a man about this and own up to what you're doing." She slammed the laptop shut and tossed it onto the chair. "I'm done. You need to leave." She brushed past him, heading for the door to show him out.

He caught her by the shoulders, stopping her in her tracks. "Wait," he said. "Baby, don't be mad. It's nothing."

Allie twisted, trying to break his grasp. "Don't 'baby' me. I'm not stupid. Let go of me."

He tightened his grip, and a whisper of unease slid along her spine. "Look, let's just go to the party, we'll have fun. Then we can go back to my place and work this all out."

Allie stilled and looked at him, and all the illusion fell away. "I don't know what I ever thought I saw in you," she said. "You aren't anybody's wish come true. You're just a shallow, self-centered man and I've given you way too many chances for no good reason at all."

There was a knock at the door. She glanced over her shoulder and then back at him. "You need to let go of me," she said. "Right. Now." And stomped on his foot as hard as she could.

With a surprised yelp, he released her and jumped back, stumbling into the Christmas tree. Ornaments crashed to the wooden floor, sending shattered glass everywhere.

The door banged open, and more hell broke loose as Chewy charged into the living room, barking like a mad thing, with Matt on his heels.

"Allie! Are you all right?" Matt called over the dog's growls as Chewy dragged him across the living room. "What's going on? I heard a crash."

Allie watched with amazement as Chewy made a beeline for Tim, backing him into a corner and keeping him there. Although he barked furiously, flinging spittle everywhere, he never touched Tim in any way.

"I'm fine," she said with a grin. "Nice timing."

"Somebody get this dog off me!" Tim's voice was high with panic as he pressed himself against the wall. Chewy stood his ground, his wet muzzle nearly level with Tim's chest.

Matt leaned close. "Don't worry. Chewy won't touch him. He'll just keep him there, away from you, until I say the word. He's kinda protective of the people he cares about."

Allie smiled up at him. The waves of care, concern and competence that rolled off of him were so tangible she felt like she could lean into them. How had she ever picked Tim over him? "Thanks, Matt. I'm really glad you're here."

"Anytime." He cleared his throat. "So, is there anything I can do for you at the moment?"

"Actually, there is. Turns out Prince Charming here is still accepting applications on MatchUp. I told him I'm out and he needs to be too. He's having some trouble taking direction. Care to help?"

Matt grinned. "Not a problem. Right, Chewy?"

"Hey, man. Call off your dog. Seriously." Tim's voice was a good octave higher than Allie had ever heard it. "I was just leaving."

Allie met Matt's gaze and nodded.

"Hey, nobody's stopping you," said Matt. He tugged gently on the leash. The dog immediately sat, but kept a focused stare on Tim. "C'mere, Chewy. You've already been fed today. We can let this one go."

"Cool. Okay." Tim sidled away from the dog and made a dash for the door. He spared a glance for Allie. "Bye," he said, and ducked out, slamming the door behind him.

She stared at the door for a moment, letting the pounding in her chest slow down. "Wow," she breathed. "That was crazy."

Matt came to stand behind her and laid his hands gently on her shoulders. It was all she could do not to lean against him and ask him to just put his arms around her for a few minutes.

"You okay?" he said. "I heard glass breaking. That's why I busted in."

"Yeah, I'm fine. Thanks for looking out for me. I'll never complain about it again." She glanced around at the mess. "I'm afraid my Christmas tree didn't do so well, though."

"The important thing is that you're okay. Ornaments are replaceable. Girls like you aren't."

Allie turned to face him. They were standing only a few inches apart, much closer than was strictly neighborly, but she didn't step back. Her heart began to pound in her ears. "Really? What about girls like me?"

Matt's gaze traveled over her face and down to her toes, as potent as a caress before he met her eye once more. "Look Allie, I'll be honest with you. I like you. A lot. A lot more than I probably should, to tell the truth. But you made it pretty clear you were interested in someone else, and I had to respect that."

"Yes, but—"

"And, God," he stabbed a hand through his hair, setting it into spikes. "It's been *killing* me to have to stand by and watch that toad-faced jerk treat you like crap for the last couple of weeks and not be able to say or do anything about it."

"Well, but—"

"And I don't want to be that guy, you know, who keeps sticking his nose where it's not wanted. I promised your brother that I'd look out for you and he's gonna be pissed about all this, but he's going to have to live with it. I can't stop thinking about you and I hope you'll give me a chance here, Allie. What do you say?"

She arched a brow at him. "You sure you're done?"

"Yeah. I'm done."

"Good," She stepped closer and wound her arms around his neck. "Because, yes," she said, and kissed him.

His arms came around her as he kissed her back. "Woo hoo!" he shouted as he lifted her off the ground and spun her around. "Merry Christmas to me!"

She laughed and kissed him again, and the dog started barking, wagging his whole body as he pranced around them in a circle. She caught a movement out of the corner of her eye and saw Phoebe under the tree, batting at pieces of things scattered across the floor.

"I'd better do something about all this broken glass," she said. "Before one of the animals gets hurt."

"I'll help." With a last lingering kiss, he released her. He walked Chewy over to the front door and made him lay down. "You stay here, boy. Don't need you walking around on glass." He turned to Allie. "Where's your broom?"

"Kitchen," she said absently, already working on righting the tree. By the time Matt had swept the floor, the tree was looking sort of restored. At least the lights were straightened.

"Hey Phoebe-kitty. What have you got there?" Allie knelt to pick up something the cat had between her paws. Tears blurred her vision as she stood. "Ohhh, what a shame." She cradled the broken pieces of the little porcelain shepardess in her hands. "This ornament's been in my family for generations. What am I going to tell my mom?"

Matt loomed over her shoulder, his presence warm and solid. "Maybe I can fix it."

"Thanks, but there aren't even enough fragments to make a good start with. Most of it is splintered. It was just too delicate." She sighed. "There goes my wish," she murmured. "Not that it did me much good anyway."

"What wish was that?"

A prickle of heat rushed to her face. "Oh, it's silly, really."

Matt zeroed in. "Oh, you're blushing. I've got to hear this."

"Well, my mom told me that when the ornament is handed to the next person in the family, they get to make a wish, and it will come true. And it was my turn."

"Did this have something to do with the guy Chewy just took care of for you?"

Her face got hotter under Matt's scrutiny. "My mom told me to be very specific."

"So you wished for a douchebag for Christmas?"

She giggled. "He kinda was, wasn't he?"

"Duh." Matt grinned. "How specific were you?"

"I wished to meet my true love that night."

Matt laughed, and shook his head. "I think your ornament's defective."

Allie shook her head. "To be fair, when I made the wish, I'd already met Tim online and he looked good. Like everything I was looking for. So, I thought the wish would be like extra insurance to help things work out, you know?"

Matt put his hands on her shoulders. "Look, I'm not saying I believe in wishes and all that. But I'm pretty sure I was the first guy at your front door that night. Remember? I was holding your cat." He gave her a smug smile. "How do you know I wasn't your wish come true?"

Allie grinned back at him. "The ornament's broken now, so I guess we'll never really know."

Matt grinned. "I don't know if I believe in all that, but one thing's for sure. You made your wish and I got mine."

She slid her arms around his waist and tipped her face up to kiss him. "Merry Christmas to me."

Jill Jaynes began her love affair with romance when she was a teenager growing up in Southern California, spending many a late-night under the covers with a flashlight and good romance novel.

This early addiction stuck, and she discovered one day that telling great stories was even more fun than reading them.

When she's not writing, you can find her a) wine-tasting, hiking or otherwise hanging out with her awesome husband, b) walking her two high-maintenance dogs, c) plotting her next story with her writer-daughter or d) working at her day job in her spare time.

Website: www.jilljaynes.com
Email: jill@jilljaynes.com
FB: facebook.com/jilljaynesromance

A Vote for Love

By Kathleen Harrington

Chapter One

December, 1886
Hanson's General Store
Helena, Montana Territory

"Now, Miss Paulie, I can't put that sign in my storefront window. Why, the folks who come in here would think I'd gone plumb crazy."

Paulette met Charlie Hanson's shrewd merchant's eyes, wide now with indignation. She smiled in reassurance. "Of course, you can put my poster in your window, sir. It's your store, isn't it?"

She fluttered her gloved fingers in exasperation, indicating the mercantile goods piled high on the counters. Wooden barrels of dried beans and rice stood nearby. Along the high wall hung rakes, shovels and brooms. The crisp scent of pine boughs emanated from the tall Christmas tree standing in one corner decorated with ornaments for sale. In the other corner stood a potbellied stove, spreading its warmth like holiday cheer.

Offering the hand-painted cardboard again, Paulette gave him an ingratiating smile. "You have every right to advertise whatever you'd like here. I'm just asking for a small favor."

Charlie stepped back as though she'd tried to shove a rattlesnake down his shirtfront. "Th-that's true. I do own this store." He ran his fingers through his thinning gray hair. "And I'm deciding I don't want no suffragette meeting advertised in my front window."

Paulette scowled but took a reluctant step back. She might have pushed a bit too hard. She had a habit of doing that.

"Does Doc Winslow know what you're up to now?" Charlie's bristly brows came together above the narrow bridge of his nose as he regarded her with obvious suspicion.

"My father is perfectly aware of my feelings on this subject, Mr. Hanson. If I asked him to, I'm sure he'd bring my poster into the store himself. And I'm certain you wouldn't be so quick to refuse *him*."

The shopkeeper raised his hands in a placating gesture. "No one in this city would refuse the doctor anything he asked, and well you know it, Miss Paulie. You just send your papa in here with one of those signs and I'll be happy to accommodate him."

"Maybe I will," she said. Knowing her father would never do any such thing, she turned with a swirl of her skirts, stomped across the rough oak floor, and swung the door of the shop open wide. "Mercy!" she muttered under her breath. "Men are impossible!"

Paulette sailed out onto the boardwalk—smack-dab into a tall stranger, who grabbed her by the elbows to keep her from falling. Her precious signs drifted to the wet boards, landing in a puddle of snowmelt.

"Watch where you're going, you big oaf!" Paulette tried to shove him away. "Now look what you've done!" Her heart sank as the paint smeared, blurring the carefully drawn posters she'd spent hours creating. Hoping to salvage something from the disaster, she bent to snatch them up.

"Whoa there, little filly!" the man said with a wide grin. He scooped the soggy cardboard pieces up in his large hands and offered them to her. His dark eyes sparkled with merriment. "No need to call me names," he continued, "though I've been called much worse in the past. And never by anyone nearly so fetching."

Paulette's breath caught high in her throat. She straightened her spectacles to peer at him, only to realize just how very handsome he appeared standing there in the afternoon sunlight. His masculine features bordered on classical perfection. The straight nose and granite chin could have been chiseled by a sculptor. Except, of course, for the thick moustache above his upper lip. No Greek statue she'd ever seen had sported facial hair.

Quite aware of her own inadequate appearance, Paulette felt the heat of a flush burn her cheeks. Far taller than the average female, she'd never enjoyed the buxom curves so admired by the opposite sex. At twenty-eight, she looked exactly like the spinster librarian she was.

"Humph," she sniffed, letting him know she couldn't be placated with a foolish compliment that no one in her right mind would believe. She snatched the signs from his grasp. *Drat it.* The wet paint stained her new leather gloves, and she smothered the urge to whack him over the head with the waterlogged paperboard.

Instead she brushed aside the broken feather that had fallen in front of her face when her hat had been nearly dislodged. And realized too late that she'd most likely smeared bright orange paint across her forehead.

The stranger belatedly swept off his wide-brimmed hat, revealing thick, black hair. The corners of his eyes crinkled with good-humor. "May I introduce myself?"

"No, you may not," Paulette snapped. She stepped around him and hurried away.

———

Brent watched the peppery redhead stride down the boardwalk, the bustle on her navy walking dress bouncing beneath the hem of her short fur-trimmed cape. She clutched her precious cargo tightly in both fists. He wondered if she'd have orange paint smeared across the front of her chest by the time she reached home. Still smiling, he entered the general store and found the owner chuckling to himself.

"I see you've met Miss Winslow," the older man said. He gestured toward the store's wide window, indicating he'd had a front-row seat to the ruckus.

"If you mean the red-haired lady, I did indeed," Brent answered with a rueful nod of his head. "I had the misfortune to knock her signs into a puddle, and she wasn't about to accept my apology."

The shopkeeper bent forward and leaned his elbows on the countertop in front of him. "Well, don't take it to heart. Paulette fires up fast, but forgives just as quickly. She ain't one to hold a grudge like some womenfolk."

"You know her well, then?"

"Yep. I've known Paulie since she was a just a mite. Her pa's the best sawbones in Helena. Don't know where she gets that wild streak from, wanting all the women in the territory to rise up and demand the vote. Must have been that female academy back East." The storeowner reached his hand across the counter. "Charlie Hanson," he said by way of introduction. "What can I do for you?"

"Brent McFarland. I'm reopening the Helena *Gazette*. I'll need to order some supplies for the printing press."

"So you're the new owner? Any relation to the McFarlands from Butte?"

"Collin McFarland is my father."

Hanson pursed his lips and gave a low whistle. "You ain't so interested in mining as your old man, I take it."

Brent shrugged, as he drew a piece of paper out of his coat pocket. He'd no intention of talking about his family's copper mines or his hard-headed father. "For the moment, I intend to concentrate on the newspaper business."

Hanson took the hint. He pointed at the paper in Brent's hand. "I'll be happy to help you with anything on your list. Let's see what you need."

———

Two days later, Paulette peered through the front window of the Gazette, trying to make out the fellow bent over the large roll-top desk in the back of the office. She'd just learned at church the previous morning that a Mr. McFarland had purchased the newspaper from its former cantankerous owner and had arrived in Helena three days earlier. One of the Copper King McFarlands, at that.

She drew in a deep breath to steady her nerves. This very office had been the scene of a rip-roaring shouting match between her and Sherman Billingsworth—a man she'd known since they were schoolchildren. How that dunce had grown into such a snide, self-important prig, she'd never know. She hoped and prayed the new owner would prove to be more open to her so-called *radical ideas*.

Steeling her backbone, Paulette opened the door and gingerly stepped inside to the noisy jangle of the cowbell announcing her arrival.

The man straightened to his full height and turned at the sound, then smiled as he moved across the room to meet her. "Well, well, Miss Winslow. To what have I the pleasure?"

The air exited Paulette's lungs in a whoosh.

Darn it! Not him!

She grasped for the first plausible excuse she could think of. "I came to apologize for my impolite behavior the other day."

"You mean outside Hanson's General Store?"

"I do."

"When you refused to allow me to introduce myself?"

"That's correct."

"After you crashed into me?" he clarified.

She hissed her answer through gritted teeth. "Yes."

"I appreciate your apology, belated as it is." His eyes sparkled, the amusement in their brown depths clearly at her expense.

Paulette lifted her shoulders in a theatrical dismissal. "Though who really crashed into whom, I'm sure I couldn't say."

"Apology accepted, Miss Winslow. And by the way, my name is Brent McFarland."

Barely inside the room, Paulette shifted from one foot to the other as she fought the temptation to step back outside, slam the door shut, and make a beeline for safety. Here, standing arms akimbo in front of her, waiting for her to go on, stood a Butte City mine owner. An honest to goodness copper king. Wealthy. Powerful. And—no doubt—ruthless.

If she stayed, she'd have to control her tart tongue. Otherwise she'd be met with a flat refusal. Debating how to go on after such a wretched beginning, she looked around the newspaper office.

Typewriters, scissors, pens, and notebooks covered most of the half-dozen beat-up desks in the large room. On cupboards along the paneled walls, stacks of old newspapers gathered dust. An enormous drafting table occupied one corner, where someone had started a layout of the *Gazette's* next edition. Other than McFarland, there appeared to be no one there. Not even in the large room at the back of the building that housed the huge printing press.

"I see you've made some new signage," McFarland said in an apparent attempt to break the awkward silence.

Paulette glanced down at the posters she clutched to her breast like a shield. "Actually, that's why I'm here," she admitted in a rush. "I have a favor to ask of you."

He raised his dark brows, clearly perplexed, then lifted a stack of books from the swivel chair in front of the roll-top desk. "Won't you sit down and tell me how I can be of service?"

Brent watched in mild curiosity as Miss Winslow stiffly took a seat, placing her hand-lettered placards on her lap. She folded her gloved hands on top of them with all the prim determination of a Bible school teacher. The broken feather on her green velvet archer's hat had been replaced by a swath of black netting gathered in a poof at the back.

Her gaze riveted on the floor in front of her, she sat ramrod straight. Behind the round, wire-rimmed spectacles, her long auburn lashes fluttered nervously. The freckles scattered across her nose and cheeks stood out like cinnamon sprinkles on her pale skin. He fought the unexpected urge to lean in closer. To reach out and follow the satiny curve of her cheek with the tip of his finger.

"Go on," he encouraged. "The worst I can do is say no."

When she looked up to meet his gaze, he recognized a flash of desperation in her wide green eyes. Clearly her mission in coming here today was of great importance to her.

"I'd like to display a poster for our coming suffragette meeting in your window," she said in a strangled voice. "If you'd be so kind as to accommodate me, Mr. McFarland," she added with a determined lift of her chin.

He straddled a nearby chair. "Please call me Brent. Surely there's no need to be so formal."

His visitor tipped her head in agreement. "Very well, Brent."

"And may I call you…?" He paused and gave her his widest, most engaging smile.

"Miss Winslow," she replied tightlipped.

"Very well, Miss Winslow, I have a proposition for you."

Frowning, she half rose from the chair, then sat back down. Her voice thick with suspicion, she inquired, "What kind of proposition?"

"I'm in need of someone to write a Sunday column for the *Gazette* about any news of interest to the female population of Helena."

"I am already employed," she informed him, her words crisp and filled with pride. "In fact, I'm on my way there now. I'm the city's librarian."

"The column would only be once a week," Brent coaxed. "And you'd likely know about most of the events without much effort on your part. I'm sure the library patrons must share their plans for upcoming luncheons and parties and fundraisers as they check out their books."

Paulette wrinkled her nose in apparent distaste. "I'm afraid not, Mr. McFarland. I haven't much interest in the latest tittle-tattle going around town. The library keeps me much too busy."

"Brent."

She gave him the smallest of smiles as she stood. "I'm afraid not, Brent."

He shrugged and rose from the ladder-back chair. Shoving it aside with the toe of his boot, he hooked his thumbs in his belt. "Then I'm afraid I can't let you display your suffragette sign in my window, Miss Winslow."

The willowy redhead sank back down with a plop. "Please call me Paulette," she insisted. "And I'll be happy to accept your offer of employment."

⸻

The next Saturday morning, Paulette entered the office of the Helena *Gazette* to find Chip Harris standing on a tall ladder and stretching his lean-limbed frame to hang an enormous Christmas wreath high on the back wall. The blond-haired young man turned his head at the jangle of the cowbell and then scampered down the rungs as agile as a monkey.

"Miss Winslow," he greeted with his big, chipped-tooth grin. "Mr. McFarland said you'd be comin' in today with your gossip column for the ladies."

Pushing back her fur-trimmed hood, she returned his infectious smile. "Hello, Chip. I'm glad to see you still have your job at the *Gazette*. When I came in here the other day, the place was deserted except for the new owner. I was afraid you'd all been replaced by someone from Butte or Anaconda."

He shook his head. "Nope. McFarland kept every dang one of us workin' the press. And I can tell you, he's a darn sight easier to work for than that tightwad, Billingsworth." Chip jerked his chin toward the large backroom of the building. The sound of whirring machinery could be heard through the open double-doors. "Wait here and I'll get the boss."

A few minutes later, Brent came into the front office, his shirtsleeves rolled up to his elbows. He smiled as he wiped his ink-stained hands on a wet rag. Apparently, he didn't leave all the manual labor to his employees. A complete contrast to the *Gazette's* previous owner.

He awarded her with a smile of approval. "Well, Miss Winslow, I'm glad to see your column's on time for the Sunday morning paper. I wasn't positive you'd be able to meet our first deadline." He tossed the soiled cloth into a wicker basket and motioned for her to sit down at a beat-up desk with a shiny new typewriter. "I had this brought in from the back especially for you. You can use it to make necessary revisions or last-minute additions. Did you have any trouble gathering enough news of interest to the ladies?"

"Not at all. It was rather easy, in fact." Remaining standing, Paulette swallowed back the lump in her throat as she offered him the first—but hopefully not last—pages of her newspaper column. "I used the typewriter we have in the library."

Brent watched the comely librarian grasp the back of the slatted wooden chair with both gloved hands. She appeared to be hanging on for dear life, as though fearing to be blown away in a gale. What the hell had she written that had left her so nervous? He glanced through the articles only to find the usual descriptions of birthday parties, school spelling bees, church socials planned for the upcoming Christmas season, and a gala ball to take place on New Year's Eve at the mayor's mansion.

On the last sheet of paper in one neat column, he found the reason for her obvious distress.

Suffragette Meeting

All the ladies of Helena are invited to attend a
meeting of the Montana Suffragette Society on
this coming Wednesday evening at the home of
Miss Paulette Winslow on 1911 Briar Street from
7:00 pm to 8:30 pm. We will discuss the upcoming election for statehood and the Montana Constitution, which MUST award WOMEN the right
to VOTE.

He looked up to meet the slender redhead's wide green eyes, filled with
apprehension, as though she expected his flat-out refusal to print it. "Well,
that's certainly of interest to the ladies," he said. "But I'm afraid I can't
publish this last article."

"You won't print my announcement?" The disappointment on her
heart-shaped face made it clear exactly which announcement she meant.

"You can hardly be surprised, Paulette. Did the former owner carry this
kind of controversial news?"

She threw back her shoulders in a defiant stance. "If you knew the former owner as well as I do, you wouldn't need to ask that question. Sherman
Billingsworth refused time and again to print anything about the suffragette
movement or women's interests, whatsoever. I suspect he doubted any of
us had the ability to read."

"Maybe that's why the *Gazette's* circulation had hit rock bottom when I
bought the paper. Still, I don't like taking the chance to find out with my
first edition."

"You're worried about your advertisers?"

"Hell, yes, I'm worried. No doubt about it. I'd be bound to lose advertisers, and they're mighty few as it is right now." Brent leaned across the
desk to plant his hands on the worn top and breathed in the fragrance of
jasmine that floated around her. For a bespectacled spinster, she had an
exotic taste in perfume. "I've sunk a lot of money into this venture. I can't
risk going belly-up over some foolish whim."

"Women's right to vote is not a foolish whim." Scowling, she snatched
the sheets of paper out of his grasp. "I'll just take my articles back, thank
you very much, and you won't print any woman's news at all tomorrow
morning."

Brent needed a column that would interest the females or he'd disap-
point half of his potential readers right out of the gate. The thought of
working closely with the vivacious redhead spurred him on, despite his

misgivings. He'd find a spot in his paper to print the invitation to the suffragette meeting. It wouldn't be on page two in her gossip column, but it would be in the paper somewhere.

He held up his hands in surrender. "You drive a hard bargain, Paulette. But I suppose we'll survive the initial shock of printing the announcement of a suffragette meeting in our first edition. We'll certainly get the attention of the entire population of Helena."

Behind the wire-rimmed spectacles, her beautiful eyes widened, astonishment in their gold-flecked green depths evident. "You'll include the suffragette meeting in tomorrow's edition?"

"I will. Your posters, however, will have to wait. Is it a bargain?" He offered his hand.

She grasped it with a wide smile, and they shook to seal the deal. "You've got yourself a bargain, sir. I'll do my best to have a great column ready for every Sunday edition."

"Now, how about having lunch with me at the café up the street?"

Her reply came out in a squeak. "Lunch? With you?"

"You do eat, don't you?"

She laughed, and the lilting sound filled the office, as clear and bright as sleigh bells on a snowy evening. "Oh, I assure you, Mr. Brent McFarland, I do, indeed!"

"Good." Brent rolled down his shirtsleeves and grabbed his jacket and hat off the hook by the door before she had a chance to change her mind. He'd negotiate the terms of her further employment over a tasty meat pie and a mug of beer. In the past, he'd never had any difficulty cajoling a pretty young female around to his way of thinking. Miss Paulette Winslow would see things his way by the end of the meal. "Let me give these pages to Chip first. We don't want to miss the morning edition."

The Bright Day Café served the best Welsh pasties in Helena. As her new employer guided Paulette toward an empty booth, the bustling place grew quiet. People craned their necks, following the path of the broad-shouldered newcomer across the black and white tiled floor.

Spotting some acquaintances, Paulette smiled and waved as she followed Brent to an empty booth. Mercy! From the stares, you'd think she'd never been seen in the company of a handsome stranger before.

Truth be told, she hadn't. Not a *handsome* stranger. Never.

Oh, she'd been accompanied many times by friends she'd known since childhood. But they'd remained exactly that. Friends.

Before they even had a chance to look at the menu, Paulette's closest confidante hurried over. Brent slid out of the booth and rose to his feet with a polite nod of greeting.

"Mr. McFarland," Paulette said, "I'd like you to meet Miss Suzy Patterson."

Suzy giggled shyly. The dimples in her plump cheeks deepened and her brown eyes sparkled. "So pleased to meet you, Mr. McFarland. Welcome to Helena. We heard that you acquired the *Gazette*. I hope you'll be happy here."

Brent smiled and took her extended hand. "How are you, Miss Patterson?"

Suzy sighed audibly. She glanced over at Paulette and lifted her brows in inquiry, her excitement fairly bubbling over. Paulette knew just what her lifelong friend was thinking—could this attractive, broad-shouldered gentleman be Paulette's new beau?

The trio was interrupted by Sherman Billingsworth, who'd entered the café a moment before and immediately stalked over to their booth. The high heels on his cowboy boots clicked on the hard floor. Paulette knew for a fact he hadn't been on a horse since he'd been tossed off at the age of nine.

"Well, McFarland," Sherman said with a sneer, tipping back an enormous Stetson which looked far too big for his head. "I see you've made the acquaintance of Helena's female rabble-rouser."

Brent barely glanced at the intruder. His reply came in a calm, quiet manner, but the deep baritone held an undercurrent of warning. "Where I come from, Billingsworth, we don't call members of the fairer gender rude names. It's considered a sign of ill breeding, if not downright cowardice. Why don't you pick on someone who can hit back?"

His face drained of color, Billingsworth took the hint, turned on his heel and moved on to another booth.

"What an obnoxious man!" Suzy whispered to Paulette. "Pay him no mind."

"Would you care to join us, Miss Patterson?" Brent asked with a warm smile.

"No, no. Thank you for the invitation, but I only came over to say hello." She squeezed Paulette's arm and dipped into a half-curtsey. "I'm sure I'll see you again soon, Mr. McFarland," she added with a little wave.

"I hope so."

Brent sat back down and favored Paulette with a sideways grin. His even teeth flashed white beneath his dark mustache. "I take it there's history between you and the former owner of the *Gazette*."

Paulette shrugged, trying hard not to reveal her true feelings. "I've known Sherman since we were schoolchildren."

"And never liked him?"

"We were never close. Let's just leave it at that."

"Gladly. Tell me about yourself. Have you lived your whole life in Helena?"

"Pretty much since the day I was born. I attended an academy in Boston for four years. Other than that I've lived in the same house on the same street. My father is one of the city's few doctors."

"And did you get your passion for women's suffrage at the academy?"

"No, I got that from my mother, who passed away two years ago. And what about you? Were you born and bred in Butte?"

Brent frowned at his menu. "I was," he replied without further elaboration. He turned to the waiter who'd come to take their order.

"The meat pies are delicious here," Paulette suggested. "You won't get better—except, perhaps, in your own hometown."

"Then shall we make it two pasties?"

"Let's."

Before Paulette had the opportunity to ask any more questions, Brent surprised her with one of his own. "I read in your column there's going to be a New Year's Eve gala. If you don't already have plans, would you allow me to escort you?"

Paulette tried to hide her surprise that this devastatingly masculine stranger would want to escort her to a ball. She'd never thought of herself as anything but plain looking and scholarly—two attributes men didn't usually find alluring.

Swallowing back a gasp of astonishment, she searched for a plausible reason for his invitation. "You want me to introduce you to Helena society?"

"That's not why I'd like to accompany you," he replied with his devil-may-care grin, "but that would be an added benefit."

"I'm planning to go with my father," she answered with a slow shake of her head. "It's one of the few festive occasions Papa attends, now that my mother is gone."

Brent reached across the table, took her hand and gently squeezed her fingers. "Perhaps I can join the two of you," he persisted, "if that would be all right with the doctor."

Paulette tilted her head and gazed into his deep brown eyes, trying to read his thoughts. A thrill of anticipation zinged through her. She tried to pull her hand away and realized it was futile. He held her imprisoned without the slightest effort.

Did Brent McFarland really want to accompany her to the ball or was there an ulterior motive? The good Lord knew, he was handsome enough and rich enough to escort any woman he chose. Her throat tightened, her heartbeat accelerated as she told herself not to get carried away. Miss Paulette Winslow, spinster, wasn't the kind of woman who turned heads as she walked down the street. But if she didn't accept his invitation, she'd never know for sure.

Throwing caution to the winds, Paulette decided to take a chance.

"I'll speak with my father this evening," she said, trying to keep from squeaking with excitement. "But I'm sure it will be fine."

To Paulette's amazement, he brought her hand to his lips. "Brave girl," he murmured. Then he sat back in the booth and the corners of his eyes crinkled as he smiled in what she could swear to be admiration. It was as though he'd read her thoughts. "I knew you had spunk, Miss Paulette Winslow, when you bumped into me and then called me an oaf. At the time, I felt lucky you didn't whack me over the head with your posters."

She returned his grin. "You don't know how lucky you were, Mr. Brent McFarland. I came within an inch of lowering the boom. You'd have been sprawled out on the boardwalk like a prizefighter kissing the canvas."

He tipped his head back and gave a shout of laughter, his rich baritone filling the room.

Cheeks burning, Paulette refused to turn and meet the startled stares of the diner's other customers.

Drat the man.

He simply brought out the worst in her.

Chapter Two

The cowbell was still jangling from its hook above the *Gazette's* door, when Brent turned to meet Paulette's furious gaze. She stood just inside the threshold, a sheet of the Sunday morning's paper clutched in her gloved hand. The tall, willowy librarian wore a long crimson wool coat trimmed in dark brown fur at the collar and cuffs. A snug fur cap covered her gorgeous red hair.

"You low-lying snake in the grass," she hissed. "You worthless, no-good trickster."

Before Brent could say a word, she balled the paper up and threw it at him. It fell to the floor at his feet where he stood beside the drafting table. Not waiting for his reply, the seething redhead charged across the newspaper office and came to a stop only inches in front of him.

"Why, Miss Winslow, whatever's gotten you so riled up on a Sunday morning?" he soothed, knowing full well the cause of her anger. "Shouldn't you be in church saying your prayers like the genteel young lady you are?"

"Don't you 'genteel young lady' me," she said through clenched teeth. Her rosy cheeks glowed, whether from the cold or her wrath, he wasn't sure. "You know very well why I'm here. You broke your word and you darn well know it."

"Tsk, tsk, such language." Brent shook his head. "And I never broke my word. I told you I'd print your invitation to the suffragette meeting in the Sunday edition and I did."

"On the back page with the paid advertisements!"

"I never said where I'd put the notice," Brent hedged. "Just that I'd print it."

Eyes narrowed, she glared at him through her wire-rimmed spectacles. "You planned this from the start, didn't you?" She fairly quivered with rage. "You're a coward, Brent McFarland." Her voice broke on the words and tears filled her eyes. "You needed a gossip column for the women readers, so you bent the truth to serve your own selfish purposes."

The sight of those tears trailing down her smooth cheeks hit him like a streetfighter's jab to the gut. "Please, try to see this from my side, Paulette," he said quietly. "I can't afford to lose advertisers. I'm just getting this paper off the ground." He touched her elbow and she jerked away. Pulling a chair from a nearby desk, Brent motioned for her to sit down. "If you'll give me a chance, I'll try to explain."

Head bent, her eyes averted, Paulette dropped slowly into the seat. She dashed the tips of her fingers, sheathed in fine brown leather, to her cheeks and brushed the tears brusquely away, as though humiliated that she'd lost her composure.

Brent sank to his haunches in front of her. Looking up into her gold-flecked green eyes, pooled now with tears, he felt an unfamiliar surge of guilt. He hadn't fully realized, until that moment, how passionate she was about the suffragette movement. How much that meeting meant to her.

"I'm sorry," he said, his words soft and reassuring. "I was wrong. I should have told you of my intention to print it as an advertisement." He took a clean white handkerchief out of his coat pocket and gently dabbed at her face.

Paulette pushed his hand away. "I'm not a baby!"

"I never thought you were." He gave her a reassuring smile. "Especially after you called me a low-lying snake. I'm just relieved that wad of paper you threw at me wasn't a knife."

She wrinkled her nose at his quiet teasing. "I should have warned you," she said with a quick, little laugh. "I have a bit of a temper."

"I kinda guessed that the first time we met." He grinned as he tugged gently on a silky red curl peeking out from under her fur cap and wound it around his calloused finger. She blushed at the intimate gesture, but didn't push his hand away. "How can I make this up to you?" he murmured.

She peered at him through her glasses, as though trying to read his intentions. "You mean, aside from promising never to pull such a nasty trick on me again?"

"Exactly," he said, placing his hand on his heart. "I promise all of your articles will be printed intact, just as you give them to me. What else can I do?"

Paulette's expression turned serious. "There is something, Brent, which I could use your help with. My father and I haven't really celebrated the holidays since my mother died two years ago. Neither of us have had the heart to decorate the house. Not so much as a holly wreath on the front door. But I think it's time now. Would you like to help me get a Christmas tree? We'd have to go into a nearby woods to find one, and it's starting to look like snowy weather is moving in."

Brent rose to his feet and drew her up with him. "You've got it. When do you want to go?"

She allowed him to hold her hands in his, but he could sense the wariness as she lifted her stubborn chin. "How about this afternoon? I'm on my way to church service now."

He chuckled, attempting to put her at ease with a bit of teasing. "After you stopped here first to berate me to my face and call me names?"

An adorable dimple peeked out in one cheek. "Well, I was planning on saying a prayer for forgiveness afterward."

"For yourself?"

"No, for you," she replied, pursing her lips. "After all, Mr. McFarland, liars and tricksters aren't allowed beyond the Pearly Gates."

Brent gave a shout of laughter. He fought the urge to gather the slender librarian into his arms and kiss the pucker right off those beautiful lips. He wasn't about to push his luck, however. He'd been granted a reprieve, but not a full pardon.

Miss Winslow wasn't like other members of the fairer sex he'd charmed into seeing things his way. This peppery female had a mind of her own. One false move on his part, and she'd give him the boot. For good.

"May I accompany you to church?" Brent squeezed her fingers, aware that he was pressing his luck to ask, but unable to keep from trying.

"Hardly!" She lifted her eyebrows in apparent dismay that he had the nerve to suggest such a thing. "People would get the wrong idea entirely."

"Then I'll see you this afternoon, Paulie." He resisted the urge to place so much as a chaste kiss on her smooth cheek and stepped back instead. "Dress warm."

Paulette gave a nod and headed to the door, where she paused to glance back at him. "This afternoon, then. You'll be able to meet my father."

Brent smiled with genuine pleasure, sensing that not many gentlemen, outside of her childhood friends, had been allowed to come calling. "I'm looking forward to it."

Brent strode up the snow-covered walkway that led to the three-story Victorian home and mounted the steps of the wide wrap-around porch. A sign next to the door read "George Winslow, M.D." When he pulled the bell, the door swung open immediately and a white-haired man smiled at him. Clearly, Brent had been expected. He was hoping for a warm reception.

"Mr. McFarland, I presume?" At Brent's nod, the slender, bespectacled man gestured a welcome. "Come in, come in, sir. I'm Paulette's father."

Brent shook his outstretched hand. "How are you, Dr. Winslow?"

"Fine, fine," he answered. "But call me George. My daughter will be down in a minute. Take off your hat and coat and let's go into the parlor while we wait. My housekeeper, Mary, will hang up your things."

A middle-aged woman, who'd been waiting nearby, dipped a curtsey and took them.

As the plump servant moved down the hall, Brent glanced around the spacious entryway, noting that a large room on the right, quiet on that Sunday afternoon, appeared to be a waiting area for the doctor's patients. He followed Paulette's father into the parlor on the left.

"Please, have a seat," the doctor said, indicating a red horsehair sofa. "I understand you two are going to find a Christmas tree this afternoon."

Brent sank onto a stiff cushion. "Yes. Paulette asked me this morning to help her."

Her father dropped into a nearby wingchair and peered at him through a pair of square, wireless eyeglasses. "Happy to hear it. It's about time we decorated for Christmas. Neither of us has been up to it since we lost Paulie's mother. I'll enjoy seeing the house bright and cheerful for the holidays once again."

"I'm more than glad to be of assistance."

Dr. Winslow picked up a pipe and tobacco pouch from a nearby side table. "Do you have some fond Christmas memories of your own?"

Brent shook his head. "None, I'm afraid." When the doctor's eyes widened in surprise, he continued. "My mother died in a coach accident when I was three. My father was far too busy with his mines to pay much attention to my five-year-old brother and me, so he left us to the care of an overworked, indifferent housekeeper. Mrs. Black had no interest in adding to her duties by putting up decorations that would have to be taken down again in a few weeks."

Refraining from any comment on the stark portrayal of the two boys' childhood, the doctor filled the bowl of his pipe and tamped it down. "Paulie tells me she's writing a woman's column for the *Gazette*," he said. "I understand you're the new owner. What made you go into the newspaper business, may I ask, when the McFarlands have always been in mining?"

"I graduated from the School of Mines in Butte." Brent had the distinct feeling Paulette's father already knew that. For good or bad, his family was well known throughout the territory. "But I'm interested in pushing for statehood and making Helena our capital. A local newspaper sympathetic to the cause might just be able get it done."

"I happen to agree with you there, Brent, though I suspect your father prefers Butte or Anaconda to be the capital, since his mining interests are there." He paused to light his pipe. "I've been asked if you can escort my daughter and me to the New Year's gala."

Surprised at the feeling of urgency welling inside him, Brent met the older man's wise, steady gaze and read the intelligence and compassion that made him such an excellent doctor. One beloved by the entire city. It suddenly seemed imperative that he gain her father's goodwill. "I would like to accompany you both, George, if that meets with your approval."

Dr. Winslow nodded, the corners of his blue eyes crinkling as he gave Brent a wide smile. "I believe it does, young man, I believe it does." He ran his fingers through his shock of white hair. "I'm pleased to see Paulie taking time for an afternoon of fun. She needs to kick over the traces a bit. My daughter sometimes takes life very seriously."

"I've noticed that." Brent couldn't repress a grin. "Especially when it comes to the suffragette movement."

"Then you don't agree that women should have the right to participate in our elections?"

"Quite the contrary. I'm all for it. But first we need to secure statehood, draw up our constitution and decide where to build our capital. There'll be plenty of wrangling over that to keep us busy for a while. We need to concentrate on getting our state laws hammered out."

Her father chuckled and puffed on his pipe. "You mean one step at a time, I take it?"

"Well, let's just say we need to keep the horse before the cart."

"Mm, I doubt my daughter will agree with you there."

Both men rose as Paulette hurried into the room. Wearing a sealskin coat trimmed in dark fur and a lush white rabbit's fur cap pulled over her ears, she met Brent's admiring gaze with a shy smile.

"And here she is now," the doctor said, beaming at his daughter. "Looking like an Eskimo dressed for the whale hunt."

"Oh, shush, Papa," she said with a lighthearted laugh as she pulled on her gloves. Her brilliant green eyes sparkled in apparent anticipation. "I was advised to dress warmly, so I suspect we're going for quite a ride."

"We'll be back well before dusk," Brent assured her father. "We're driving up toward Helena Mountain, but we won't go far. Just far enough to pick out the tallest, straightest pine in the forest." He glanced up at the room's high ceiling. "Well, maybe not the tallest, but a nicely shaped one. I promise, you'll need a ladder to put a star on the top."

The doctor clapped Brent on the shoulder with a hearty laugh. "I'll bring in the ladder while you're gone."

"No need to do that today. I'll stash the tree on your porch for the night and be over in the morning to put it up before heading to the newspaper office."

George walked them to the door, where the housekeeper waited with Brent's heavy coat and hat. "You two have fun."

"We will, Papa." Paulette gave her father a little wave before stepping out onto the porch alongside her broad-shouldered escort. A shiver of excitement coursed through her at the sight of the shiny red sleigh, trimmed in black and drawn by a pair of matching chestnuts. "Why, they're magnificent!"

"I'm glad you think so." She could hear the pride in Brent's deep baritone. "I had them brought over from Butte in easy stages. They arrived with the sled yesterday."

He took her elbow and led her down the steps.

Paulette hurried over to pat their soft, quivering noses. "What are their names?"

"Ruby has the splash of white on her forehead. The other is Rosebud." He flashed her a dazzling grin. "I've always been partial to redheads."

A flush burned Paulette's cheeks, but before she could say a word, he swung her up into the sleigh and bundled a thick blanket around her. The sturdy soles of her fur-lined winter boots rested on a heated brick. Cozy and warm, she breathed in the fresh still air, as a tingle of breathless excitement raced down her spine.

Brent moved to the far side of the sleigh, where he paused to check the Winchester rifle stowed in its scabbard by his seat before climbing in.

"Planning on doing some hunting?" she asked.

"If we spot a deer, we could have venison for Christmas dinner. Hold on." He slapped the reins and gave a sharp whistle. The team took off to the sound of jingling harness bells as the runners skimmed over the snow.

"I've always wanted to whistle like that," she admitted with a sigh of nostalgia. "No matter how hard I tried when I was a girl, I could never get it right."

"It's just a matter of practicing the placement of your lips and tongue. I'd be happy to help you learn."

Paulette smothered a gasp. She peeked at Brent from the corner of her eye, but he seemed unaware of how inappropriate his offer sounded to a spinster librarian. He held the reins lightly in one gloved hand, his gaze fastened on the road out of Helena. A thrill of joy zinged through her. She buried her nose in her fluffy white muff to hide a secret smile.

Mercy, the man was a rogue and a flirt!

And didn't she just love it!

In the afternoon sun, the snow-covered hills sparkled with the brilliance of diamonds. The pine forest rose up like a dark green smudge against the clear blue Montana sky. Exhilaration surged through Paulette, setting her heart pounding to the rhythm of the horses' hoofs on the hard-packed snow.

Brent and Paulette weren't the only ones in search of a suitable Christmas tree that day. When their sled drew to a stop in a dense stand of evergreens, Suzy Patterson and several other young people could be seen on the slope above, watching Chip Harris, the *Gazette's* office manager, chop down a fat spruce laden with snow on its branches.

The lively brunette waved to the newly-arrived pair, then tramped across the snow to their sleigh. "We're going to Ming's Noodle Palace for supper before taking the tree to my house. The food's already been ordered. Come with us!" Her plump cheeks rosy from the cold, her brown eyes aglow, she smiled entreatingly.

Having no intention of upsetting Dr. Winslow, Brent raised his brow. "What do you say, Paulie?" he asked, coming around to her side of the sleigh. "Will your father be worried about you?"

Before she could answer, Suzy waved to another friend on horseback, who immediately waved back. "Neil isn't able to join us for dinner. We'll be taking his tree back with us. I'm sure he can stop by and tell your papa our plans on his way home."

Paulette rested her gloved hands on Brent's shoulder as he lifted her down from the sled. "As long as I'm not too late and I'm with friends, I'm sure it will be fine with Papa." She tipped her head back to meet Brent's gaze, and her long auburn lashes fluttered in her apparent hesitation. "If it's convenient for you, of course. I'm already taking up your time this afternoon."

He grinned in pleasure at the thought of escorting her to dinner. "I have no plans for the evening. My time is yours."

Behind him, Suzy giggled with infectious good humor. "Well, hurry and get a tree. We're practically ready to go."

True to his word, Brent was determined to search for the perfect Christmas tree to fit in the Winslow parlor.

"This one's pretty," Paulette said, pointing to a conifer near the roadside.

He shook his head as he led her away from the sleigh and into the woodland. "Too sparse and not nearly tall enough."

"What about that one?" she asked, pointing to a thick-branched pine.

"We can do better than that." Bracing his axe on his shoulder, Brent grabbed Paulette's hand and tugged her along as he moved farther uphill. "I've spotted a beauty on the top of the rise."

They tromped through the snow, laughing when she fell into a drift. Dropping the axe, Brent pulled her up. He brought her close and met her startled gaze.

"I'm perfectly fine," Paulette said in a breathless voice. She braced the palms of her gloved hands on his chest as though to push away.

"I couldn't agree more, angel," he said, relishing the scent of jasmine that surrounded her. "You're damn near perfect."

In their nearness, her spectacles clouded as their warm breaths mingled. He held her for the space of a second longer, then reluctantly released her, well aware of the audience brimming with curiosity just downhill.

After cutting down the finest evergreen on the slope, Brent lashed it to the back of his sleigh. He looked up just in time to duck a snowball whizzing by his head. Suzy and Chip, along with several others, were advancing toward them, snowballs cradled in their arms.

Paulette gave a happy shriek and bent to grab some snow. "Quick!' she called to him. "Arm yourself! It's a sneak attack!"

Brent was doing just that. He lobbed his first missile with such force, he knocked his grinning office manager on his butt in a pile of snow.

Paulette stood right beside Brent, her aim excellent, if not as powerful as his. They withstood a fusillade of white cannonballs, giving as good as they got, everyone howling with excitement until both sides dropped to the ground, panting and gasping for breath.

Brent looked over to see Paulette fling herself, arms wide, onto the snowy bank, her face turned to the sky, her laughter filled with pure happiness.

So the spinster librarian knew how to play with abandonment.

A fleeting image of her lying on his bed, her beautiful eyes meeting his in the glow of a candle, sent the blood rushing through his veins.

As a schoolboy, he'd been told never to judge a book by its cover.

When it came to Miss Paulette Winslow, truer words had never been spoken.

Chapter Three

Paulette and her friends had eaten at Ming's Noodle Palace often. They had developed a fondness for Oriental cuisine. Decorated in lavish peacock feathers and gilded masks, the noodle parlor was one of Helena's most popular eateries. As they waited by the door, she looked around to see Mr. Wong, the restaurant's owner, making his way toward them.

Dressed in a lavishly embroidered silk jacket with a high collar, Wong had a black skullcap on his head and his braided queue fell all the way down his back.

"Welcome to my humble establishment. It is good to see everyone again." He pressed his palms together in front of his chest and bowed low, and then turned with polite curiosity to the tall stranger in their midst.

"Mr. Wong, this is the *Gazette's* new owner, Mr. McFarland, from Butte," Paulette said.

An unconscious air of authority and wealth seemed to radiate from the able-bodied newcomer, and Wong bowed again, this time more deeply. "It is a great honor, sir." With a wide smile, he gestured for the high-spirited group to follow him. "Come this way, please. I have a large table in the far corner that will accommodate all of you."

The interior of Ming's Noodle Palace shimmered beneath a rainbow of light from the Chinese lanterns of blue and green and red hanging from its low ceiling. Screens of rice paper, embellished with gold celestial symbols, divided the spacious room into cozy alcoves for the guests. When Brent gently placed his hand on the small of Paulette's back and guided her through the room, her chest swelled with pride. More than one female stared in open-mouthed envy at her handsome escort, as they followed the dignified proprietor through a maze of tables filled with patrons.

With consummate grace, Wong pulled three chairs out for the ladies, while the men took all the coats and hats and gave them to an attendant nearby. Then he clapped his hands and a waiter in black silk pajamas hurried over. "See that my friends have everything they want."

After the snowball fight on the mountain, Paulette had introduced Brent to Margaret Telford and her beau, Fredrik Vasa. Suzy and Chip had ridden with the couple in Freddie's large sledge, loaded with three thick pines and pulled by a team of sturdy farm horses.

Once the wine was poured, the waiters brought bowls of egg-drop soup, followed by platters of chicken with almonds and snow peas, mounds of fried rice and shrimp, along with wonton and pots of hot tea.

During the meal, the topic inevitably turned to the coming election. Everyone at the table agreed that Montana should become a state and Helena its capital. The close-knit group of friends expressed their surprise, however, when Brent agreed, since his family owned mines in Butte and Anaconda.

"I plan to write an editorial in the coming Sunday edition," he told them. "In fact, that's why I purchased the newspaper here in Helena, where I hope our state representatives will meet in the future."

"And what about the vote for women?" Margaret inquired. Blond and buxom, she tilted her head, meeting their gazes with a hesitant smile. "Shouldn't we be allowed to cast our ballots?"

"Pooh! Why bother to give women the vote?" Freddie looked to the other men for agreement. "Wives will simply vote like their husbands advise them."

"Not necessarily!" Paulette dropped her chopsticks on her plate and glared at the muscular Swede. "If a woman disagrees with her husband, she can make her own decision. She has a mind of her own."

"Yes!" Suzy exclaimed, as though she'd never thought of the idea till that moment. Her brown eyes sparkled, and the dimples on her cheeks deepened. "After all, the voting is done in secret."

"I'm not sure." Chip frowned, shaking his head. "Women don't know much about finance or business in general. What would they know about runnin' a country?" He turned to his employer. "What do you think, Boss?"

"I think we've hit on a touchy subject," Brent replied. "Maybe we'd better talk about the weather or the latest women's fashions." He smiled at the ladies, trying to lighten the mood. "I hear bustles will be back again in the spring."

"Oh, come on!" Margaret waved her hand with persistence. "Surely you have an opinion."

Brent leaned back in his chair, all eyes upon him. "I think women should be given suffrage. Eventually. Right now, we need to put our energy into choosing a capital and drawing up a constitution."

The outrage in Paulette's voice was unmistakable. "Then women don't have the commonsense to help craft our state laws?"

Damn.

Just the argument Brent wanted to avoid. He'd been looking forward to the ride home with his lovely companion. Something told him that romantic ride home was about to be spoiled.

He kept his tone even and patient. "Not at all. But I think female suffrage should be put on the backburner for now. We need to prioritize our goals and work on the most attainable ones first."

"And how long must we wait?" Paulette's thick-lashed eyes narrowed in annoyance. "Five years? Ten? A lifetime?"

Before he could answer, the rustle of a commotion spread through the restaurant. Everyone looked over to see Sherman Billingsworth swaggering his way through the tables, a garishly painted harlot on his arm.

Brent suddenly realized why the *Gazette* had been foundering when he bought it. He'd assumed that the men of this rough-and-tumble former gold camp had cancelled the newspaper, along with many of its advertisers, because they disagreed with its political leanings. He couldn't have been more wrong.

Every wife and mother in Helena must have demanded that the newspaper's subscription be dropped. Not because of its editorials. Nor its lack of a ladies' column. By bringing a prostitute to a family restaurant on a Sunday evening, the former owner showed a basic lack of common decency. Billingsworth must have scandalized the city's upper-crust in the past, and its more genteel inhabitants had turned against him.

When Brent looked back at his table partners, he could see the condemnation on their faces. The men scowled. The ladies averted their eyes, as though pretending not to have noticed.

The mood had definitely soured.

The meal was over.

It was time to leave.

As they rose from their chairs, Paulette gave him a weak half-smile. "I can ride home with the others, Mr. McFarland. It's really on their way, and you won't be troubled to go out of yours."

Brent's clipped words made it clear he had no intention of arguing about it. "I promised your father I'd return you safely home, my dear. I always keep my promises."

Before she could say another word, he bundled Paulette into her sealskin coat and steered her toward the front door.

———

The couple rode in silence behind the prancing chestnuts. While the friends had dined, the horses had been taken to a nearby livery, where they were watered, fed and covered with warm blankets. Now the animals were restless and ready to cover ground, so Brent allowed them a fast trot. Beside him, Paulette sat stiff and clearly unhappy, her jaw clenched, her gaze fastened on the road ahead.

The sleigh skimmed over the snow, the harness bells jingling in the crisp air. Overhead, the Milky Way, with its countless stars, lit up the black winter sky.

"It's a lovely night," he offered, trying to start a friendly conversation.

"I hadn't noticed."

"Try to understand my side, Paulette," he said. "I refused to dissemble or mislead, just to please you or anyone else at the restaurant. I have to say and do what I believe is right."

She tossed her head for dramatic emphasis and sniffed. "Hmph. I feel the exact same way. And to be perfectly honest, Mr. McFarland, I don't like you. How's that for plain-speaking?"

He chuckled in an attempt to lighten the tone. "Right at the moment, you're not being too likeable yourself, sweetheart. But I'm willing to overlook it."

"I'm not your sweetheart!" She turned to glare at him, and then clamped her mouth shut, refusing to say another word.

When they drew up in front of her home, Paulette didn't wait for Brent to come around to her side of the sleigh. She jumped down and raced up the pathway. By the time they neared the door, Brent was right behind her. He reached over her shoulder and pulled the bell.

Papa opened the door with a smile, then stepped back to let his daughter hurry inside. "Everything all right?" he asked, looking from one to the other with a frown.

"We had a little disagreement," Brent explained. "About politics."

"Ah," her father said. "I think I understand." Lifting his brow, he looked at his daughter again. "Where are your manners, Paulie? Aren't you going to thank the gentleman and tell him goodnight?"

Squaring her shoulders, Paulette folded her arms across her chest and met Brent's gaze. *"Good-bye!"* She had the satisfaction of slamming the door in the exasperating man's face before bursting into tears.

Her father put his arms around her and held her close. "What's wrong, child?"

"Oh Papa," she wailed. "I think I'm in love with that horrible man."

Chapter Four

Eight days later, Paulette glanced around the Helena Public Library to make sure everything was in order before picking up the lantern by the front desk. A dull ache pressed on her chest as she searched for the building key in her purse. The unhappiness sitting on her shoulder like a morose black crow had been her constant companion since the disastrous evening at the noodle parlor.

She heard the high front door swing open and turned, about to tell the latecomer that the library was already closed.

Brent McFarland stepped inside. His broad shoulders seemed to fill the doorframe. He loomed even taller than the last time they spoke. Beneath his dark brown moustache, his mouth was set in a firm line.

"You-you-you're too late," she stuttered. Her voice sounded weak and filled with the heartache she'd been trying so hard to hide from the world. "I'm just about to lock up."

"I know. I came to drive you home."

"That's not necessary. I always walk. It's only five blocks. Just a nice stretch of the legs."

His granite chin came up and he scowled at her. "It's already dark outside, Paulie. You won't be able to see the pathway."

"I'll take the lantern with me as I always do." Still rifling around in her bag, she forced a smile. The sinking feeling in her stomach warned her that Brent wasn't a man to take no for an answer once he'd made up his mind. If he intended to take her home, he'd take her home.

Brent pulled off his winter hat and leather gloves and laid them on her desk, making it clear that he had all the time in the world to wait for her to come around to his way of thinking. He looked slowly about the library, as though curious to see the place where she spent most of her days.

Where she'd been hiding out for over a week.

Paulette followed his gaze to the evergreen garlands, colorful glass balls, and red satin ribbons decorating the tops of the bookshelves. She'd used some of the bottom branches of the spruce he'd cut for her on the mountainside to brighten the library for Christmas. Her mother's painted Nutcrackers stood in a row on a narrow table nearby, along with a carved wooden crèche.

"Thank you for setting up the tree for Papa the morning after…" The words trailed off in her embarrassment. She'd made certain she left for the library before Brent arrived that day. And she'd handed her next Sunday column to Chip on his way to the newspaper office on Saturday morning.

"You're welcome. I was hoping I'd be invited back to help put the decorations on the tree."

Paulette swallowed back a painful lump. Her father had told her about Brent's lack of childhood Christmas memories. When she tried to speak, her words came out in a croak. "Considering our conflicting views, I didn't think… I don't think now…"

"I've had the feeling you've been purposely avoiding me," Brent interrupted, as though he'd been reading her thoughts. "I waited till all your customers left so we could discuss our so-called conflicting views."

"Library patrons." Paulette managed a half-hearted smile. At his quizzical look, she added, "We call them patrons."

"Of course."

Dear God, why didn't the dratted man just go and leave her to her misery? Paulette bit her lower lip to keep back the tears. She would never stop fighting for women's right to vote. She wasn't going to be silenced. And she wasn't willing to wait. Not another year. Not even six months. At Ming's Noodle Palace, he'd made it perfectly clear where he stood on that issue.

"I came to give you an early Christmas present, Paulie."

The hushed timbre of Brent's words seemed to spark a fire inside her.

"I couldn't accept a gift from you!" Dressed in her long winter coat, she propped her hands on her hips, making no attempt to hide her disapproval. "It wouldn't be proper. Why, we barely know each other."

"I believe this is one present you'll be willing to accept." He edged closer, as though worried she might panic and bolt. "I'd like you to write an article for the Opinion Section in the *Gazette's* Christmas edition next week. I want you to logically and factually set forth all the reasons why women should be given the vote. And I want you to persuade the men of Helena that the time is now."

When Paulette stood frozen with astonishment, he moved even closer. Happiness rocketed through her. Without thinking, she threw her arms around his neck, intending only a grateful hug. He immediately brought her against him and lifted her up till they were nose to nose. She drew a shaky breath and inhaled the spicy aroma of shaving soap. The sudden yearning to watch him strop his razor and run its sharp blade carefully across his thick morning beard tantalized her.

She pushed back, her hands braced on his muscular shoulders. "Wait a minute! Are you doing this because you agree with me or because you like me?"

"A little of both." He nuzzled her neck just below the ear and she shivered involuntarily.

Paulette fought the startling sensations that seeped through her. She leaned back to meet his gaze, unable to keep the disappointment from her voice. "You only like me *a little*?"

Beneath his thick mustache, his even white teeth flashed in his devil-may-care grin. "Okay, I'll admit it." His deep baritone came low and husky. "I was smitten the day we met, Miss Winslow, when you threatened to whack me over the head with your suffragette posters. I'd never met anyone like you before, a gorgeous red-haired Valkyrie, quivering with righteous indignation."

Setting her back on her feet, he cupped the back of her head in his hand. He bent and gently took her lower lip between his, tugging softly, then nibbled seductively on her upper lip, as though silently coaxing her to respond.

"So you'll do it?" he murmured.

Surrendering all doubt, Paulette released a long, low sigh. "I will."

Brent placed a finger beneath her chin, lifting her face closer to his. A budding excitement surged through her. Until that moment, she had never experienced a sensual kiss—only a chaste buss from a would-be beau. Instinctively, she knew this powerful, self-assured man would be an experienced lover. She hoped he wouldn't be disappointed, but she was willing to throw caution to the winds and find out.

With her face cradled between his large hands, Brent covered her mouth with his. Paulette returned his passionate kiss without a moment's hesitation.

———————

The New Year's Eve gala brought out all of Helena's society matrons, along with their husbands attired in formal evening dress and attached securely on their arms. Given by the city's mayor and his wife, the festive gathering took place in their redbrick mansion. The entire second floor had been cleared for the dancing and was now filled with the lilting strains of a Viennese waltz.

As Brent guided his beautiful partner around the polished oak floor, he met her gold-flecked green eyes, shinning now with happiness. They'd come to the ball with Paulette's father, but once they'd reached the dance floor the couple had eyes only for each other.

Brent had attended Christmas services with Paulette and her father. Then he spent the day at their home. He'd given her a set of mother-of-pearl combs for her magnificent hair, and her obvious delight with his gift had filled him with a new-found Christmas joy. A feeling he'd never known as a child. A joy he'd make certain every child of his own would know.

At the moment, George stood talking to a group of older men, but every so often he'd glance their way, beaming with pleasure. Earlier in the evening, Brent and the white-haired doctor had shared a very important conversation in the Winslow parlor before Paulette came downstairs, ready to go to the ball.

Clearly, Paulette loved to dance. She hummed softly to the music as Brent whirled her in the waltz. She wore a gown of emerald silk that skimmed her creamy shoulders. Her gorgeous mahogany curls were piled high on her head and fastened with those mother-of-pearl combs. Emerald green ribbons secured three fat ringlets at her neck, along with a cluster of fragrant gardenias. If she didn't look like a red-haired angel, no one ever had. Gazing at her now, Brent's heart seemed to overflow with happiness.

When the dance came to an end, he led her off the floor. "Let's go downstairs and get some fresh air," he suggested.

"Should we check on Papa first?"

"I saw George talking with his friends a moment ago. They probably went to join in a game of billiards in the back parlor. I'm sure he's fine."

Together they descended the ornate staircase, decorated with garlands and red velvet ribbons. A giant chandelier cast a glow over the landing. Everywhere Paulette looked bright red candles burned in hurricane lanterns. Evergreen branches tied with gold bows adorned all the transoms.

Trying to hide her girlish captivation, Paulette peeked at her handsome escort from the corner of her eye. In a black tuxedo and tie, Brent McFarland exuded power and wealth and raw male sensuality. A tingle of excitement spread through her at the thought that he'd chosen to accompany her to the ball.

Brent led her out onto a wide veranda, where they stood beside its carved white railing and gazed up at the wide Montana sky. The night was clear and still. Moonlight lit the snowy landscape. Brent stood behind her, his strong arms encircling her with his warmth.

Paulette rested her head on his shoulder and released a long, drawn-out sigh. "I feel as though I could almost reach out and touch the moon. It seems so brilliant in the black velvet sky, like a gigantic Chinese lantern."

"You sound very happy," he murmured in her ear. The timbre of his baritone vibrated against her back, sending a thrill pinging down her spine.

She turned in his arms to face him. "Oh, Brent, I've never been so happy."

He smiled as he took her hands. "Let's keep it that way, sweetheart. For I've never been happier either. I want to spend the rest of my life assuring your happiness."

To her astonishment, Brent took a small black velvet container out of his inner coat pocket and dropped to one knee on the wooden porch. He opened the jewelry box, and she gasped at the largest diamond she'd ever seen.

Kathleen Harrington

"Miss Paulette Winslow, will you do me the honor of becoming my wife?"

Paulette dropped to her knees in front of him, her full-skirted ball gown billowing about her like a silken jade cloud. "Oh, yes!" Tears of happiness spilled from her eyes. "Oh, my darling, yes!"

Her entire body trembled as he took her left hand and gently slid the ring onto her finger.

Holding each other's hands, they rose to their feet together. "I love you, Paulie," he said, his words thick and hoarse. Kissing her forehead, the tip of her nose, and each cheek, he repeated, "I love you, I love you, I love you."

"I love you so much, Brent." She brushed the tip of one trembling finger across his thick moustache.

Drawing her into his embrace, he covered her mouth with his in a long, lingering kiss.

From inside the mansion, an enormous grandfather clock struck midnight and a cheer arose from the partygoers. The refrain of "Auld Lang Syne" floated through the air.

"Happy New Year, darling," he murmured.

Paulette's heart seemed to swell in her chest with pure joy. "Happy New Year, my love," she whispered, lifting her mouth to his.

Kathleen Harrington, multi-published, award-winning author, has touched the hearts of readers across the country and the world with her sparkling tales of high adventure and unending love. Her historical romances have been published in Chinese, Russian, Italian, and German. She lives in Southern California with her American Bulldog, Auron.

www.kathleenharringtonbooks.com

Night Train to Hong Kong

by Ottilia Scherschel

On the night of December 18, the high-speed train waited in Beijing's main station. Sarah Crawford, washed along by the crowd, moved toward a brightly lit platform. Balancing a rolling bag and tucking an oversized purse close to her body, she passed a Santa in full costume jamming on a saxophone. She smiled at this odd take on Christmas and trudged up a few steps to board a type of train she had never ridden.

The attendant glanced at her ticket and passport before directing her down the corridor to her luxury soft sleeper whose door had been left open in welcome. She entered and slid it shut. The inside space was tight. She shoved her bag under the lower berth that was already made up with clean bedding for sleeping. On the opposite wall, an armchair snuggled in a niche next to the private bathroom's door. She stashed her purse in a shallow closet behind the chair. On the wall opposite the entry, a table stood below a large window.

"Hardly luxurious but not bad for a last-minute Plan B." She found comfort in expressing her thoughts out loud, comfort in having found a way home, comfort in being able to keep her promise to be with her aging parents for the holidays.

When she sat to test the mattress, the train rocked a little and slid over the rails on schedule at 8:10 p.m. The smooth movement and the silence in the compartment surprised her. If she didn't know better, she would have sworn she was on an airplane. Her worries about being able to sleep vanished. Her private cocoon was perfect.

Two quick taps on the door drew her attention. She slid it open.

A man wearing jeans and a classic navy zip-front jacket stepped over the threshold. "Hi! We're compartment mates."

For a heartbeat her breath stalled. "What?" Pulling her ticket from a pocket of her black travel pants, she reached out and stuck it under his nose. "You sure?"

He looked at it beside his own. "That's it, our compartment." His mouth stretched into a straight line, signaling his firm conviction.

"You read Chinese?"

"Yes." He moved closer and extended a hand. "Evan Murphy."

"Sarah Crawford." She gave him the limp fish shake. "But there's some mistake. I know I paid for a single." She stared up at him. He stood a few inches above her five nine and age-wise had to be somewhere near her thirty-one.

"That's possible," he said, "but I was sold the other berth."

He flashed a crooked smile that, coupled with his dark hair and intense gunmetal blue eyes, made him more appealing than she was willing to admit, especially under these awkward circumstances. "Let's have an attendant straighten this out."

"There aren't any in this car," Evan Murphy announced.

She huffed out a breath. "One checked my ticket."

He backed out, squeezing his swimmer's shoulders through the narrow opening.

She peeked into the corridor. A few passengers shuffled along with their bags, but there was no sign of help.

"Couldn't we work this out?" he asked. "The train is fully booked."

"Really?" The last thing she wanted was some stranger in her compartment.

"It's the Winter Solstice. Like at home at Christmas, everyone travels to see family. It's a tradition." He spoke in a gentle tone and had those dark Irish good looks that made her smile and want to believe every word he uttered.

She blinked. "I still want to speak to an attendant." She was determined to have this go her way.

"All right." He raised a carry-on in the air. "May I?" he asked, stepping within inches of her.

She sensed his heat and the scent of his minty aftershave and continued to fight the attraction. "For now." She backed into the compartment.

He tossed his one piece of luggage on the fresh linen of the berth where she planned to sleep. "I'll look for the attendant," he said, leaving and closing the door.

Damn! She had no plan C, and no idea of how to get rid of Evan who threatened the possibility of a good night's sleep and her privacy. She was not up for this intrusion. But after two weeks of working on her first assignment in China, she had learned she had to be patient and flexible. The latter, she could handle, but patience was never easy.

She turned on the volume to the intercom. Chinese music wafted through the cubicle. She had discovered the unusual sounds of the stringed instruments had an ethereal quality that soothed her ruffled edges. She dug her water thermos out of her purse and sipped slowly, wishing for something more potent to relax her. As she parked the container on the table, the double tap sounded again.

She slid the door open. "Did you forget something?"

Instead of Evan, another stranger rushed in. Without a word, he shoved her in the ribs. She stumbled backwards, sucking in air with a loud wheeze. "Ugh," she groaned as the air rushed out of her. Pain shot through her ribcage.

The intruder jerked the compartment door shut.

She was trapped. Her frantic heartbeat thundered in her chest.

The stocky man with a moon face took two menacing steps toward her. "Where is it?" he bellowed. The overhead light cast fearsome shadows across his face. His thick lips hung slightly open. His breath reeked of garlic and his body of cologne, sweet like orange blossoms.

Her knees went weak. She gaped at him. "Where's what?"

"Don't play dumb." He pushed her aside, flat against the closed bathroom door, and grabbed Evan's carry-on from the berth.

"Leave that," she yelled.

With his free hand, he shoved her against the table. Turning sideways in the tight space, he moved toward her. He had to be as wide as her refrigerator.

A primal instinct made her reach behind her for the thermos. "No," she cried out, hitting him with all the force she could muster.

The man moaned. He fingered his thick black hair at the crown.

Before she knew what was happening, he was on her, pinpoint eyes glaring, his body boxing the narrow aisle, blocking the only exit.

His hand shot out and vise-gripped her wrist. She kicked and clawed, trying to pull out of his grasp. "Let me go!" she shouted. He dropped the bag and dragged her forward. Positioning himself behind her, he braced her body with his and twisted her arm against her spine.

Pain shot to her shoulder, burning every muscle on the way. She whimpered and stopped resisting, but he wrenched it harder. The ache intensified. He thrust her the few feet toward the bathroom door. Her shins grazed the edge of the berth on the way, bruising flesh.

With brute force, he pushed her inside the bathroom and banged the door shut between them.

She stood in the dark, her body shaking and her lungs heaving as she gasped for air. She feared she would collapse in a heap, feared the intruder would come back. She ran her hands over the wall. Her fingers found the light switch. The brightness of the fluorescents on either side of the mirror blinded her for a moment. Taking a deep breath, she sat down on the toilet lid. What had just happened?

Nothing good. She had never been in danger like this before and never wanted to be again. And for what? *It.* She had no clue what *it* could be.

Rolling her aching shoulder, she stretched her arm. Everything worked, but her wrist was reddened from being squeezed, and her shins promised black and blue marks.

She had to get out of this hideous situation. Standing, she put an ear to the door. Not a sound. Grasping the door lever, she pushed up and down. The lever shifted in neither direction.

Fisting a hand, she pounded the door while yelling for help at the top of her voice.

Where was Mr. Crooked Smile when she needed him? Crooked. What instinct made her conclude that? Was Evan the cause of her problem? The intruder had taken his carry-on.

A clatter outside brought her back to reality. The door opened. The high-pitched strains of a Chinese opera preceded Evan who now stood before her. It was almost a ridiculous "ta-da" moment.

"You all right?" he asked.

Sarah narrowed her eyes. "No," she squealed. "Someone tried to kill me."

"Are you hurt?" He looked her up and down.

"Pissed." She charged toward the armchair, stopping to pick up the water thermos from the floor on the way. "I hit him with this." She waved the thermos in the air.

"Who?"

"The Chinese goon. Got him in the head. He was furious, ready to slit my throat."

"He had a knife?" Evan's eyebrows rose along with the volume of his voice.

"No, he pushed me around, twisted my arm and locked me in the bathroom." To her surprise the words poured out of her as if she couldn't wait to tell someone. "Call security."

Evan flicked off the intercom. After taking the thermos from her hand, he pushed a couple of strands of hair off her face and behind her ear. His gaze softened. "Try to calm down."

Her legs weak, she plopped in the armchair. To her right, a deep gash cut the wall. "Why's the tabletop on the berth?"

"Someone used it to wedge the bathroom latch." He put down the thermos and moved the top to make a spot to sit. "Tell me what happened," he added in a soothing tone.

Sarah hesitated. Then, her pulse rate picked up. She started from the moment she unlocked the compartment door thinking Evan was knocking.

Leaning toward her, he looked directly at her.

Her story came in short bursts of words that accelerated her breathing. When she came to the end, she inhaled and exhaled, trying to moderate the adrenaline surging through her. Was she having a panic attack? She didn't know. She had never had one.

He cleared his throat. "What did the thug say he wanted?"

"It!" Sarah said. "Just *it*."

"Where is the souvenir you bought?"

"How do you know I bought one?" She crossed her arms over her chest. The muscles in her injured arm and shoulder ached. Her shins burned. "Who the hell are you?"

"Look, I'm going to be straight with you. I'm a private investigator."

"And I'm on the Orient Express."

He grinned. "I track stolen artifacts, Chinese antiquities specifically."

"You're serious."

"I've been working on a smuggling case for the past six months. A couple of weeks ago, an informant put me on to a Beijing dealer who uses unsuspecting tourists to sneak objects into the States."

"The place where I shopped?" She uncrossed her arms.

"Actually…"

"You've been following me." Heat scorched her cheeks at the idea she'd been used.

"Only since you went in the store. My informant told me the first tourist shopping that morning would be given an item. He signaled as you left that you were that person."

Guys had told her a lot of bull, but this was a new one. "Do you have some ID? Something to back up your crazy story."

He fished out his wallet and handed over a calling card and a copy of a California PI license.

She studied the proof. "My friend bought one of these licenses online for a costume party. How do I know yours isn't a fake?"

"You can email my firm to verify."

"I could, but I'd rather report the attack to security."

"Would you hear me out first?" His voice was mellow, warm and buttery. Curious enough to listen, she blew out a breath and said, "Okay."

"So far, I partly know how this smuggling ring works, but you're my key to figuring it out from beginning to end."

"What do you mean?"

"I know how artifacts are planted on tourists. I don't how the smugglers get to the artifacts once the objects arrive at their destination. By following you, I intended to solve that end of the puzzle."

"But if I have something that needs smuggling, why was I attacked?"

His voice rumbled through the compartment. "That's the million dollar question."

"So train security can catch my attacker, and you can interrogate him and find out."

"Security will turn the train inside out and hang us up for days. In the end, they won't let a foreign PI question anybody, and they certainly won't share information with one."

"I can't have another delay." She looked out the window at night-lights streaking past. "I'm on this train because a work issue made me miss a direct flight home. I won't change my travel plans again." She had never missed spending Christmas with her parents. Disappointing them was no-where on her to do list.

"Then, you'll help me find this thug."

"You can find him?"

"I make my living finding people and getting information. I'm trained in close quarter combat and did two tours in Afghanistan."

She scrutinized his broad shoulders, muscular arms and close-cropped hair. The Rolex on his left wrist confirmed he made a good living. Part of her wanted to throw in with him and another part wondered if she should believe him.

That smile tugged at the corner of his mouth. "How about we send the email to verify who I am?"

Confirmation was what she needed. "Let's," she said.

He pulled his phone from his pocket. "I'll set up an outgoing message, and you can type what you want in the body."

She glanced at his card and checked the outgoing address for a match. Satisfied, she entered her questions before pushing send. "No signal." She would be sure to check later to see if the email went out.

"Tell me one thing," she said, handing him the phone. "Why did the guy take your suitcase and not mine?"

"Because it was in plain sight," he said, shrugging his shoulders. "Where is yours?"

"Under you."

He stood and put her black rolling bag on the berth.

"What am I supposed to have?" She stood next to him.

"What did you buy?"

She unzipped the bag. After digging around, she pulled out a baseball-sized round of tissue and unwrapped a small statue. She shook her head. "The clerk went in the back to wrap my purchase. This isn't what I bought." She laid it in his outstretched palm. "What is it?"

"A Pixiu," he answered. "An animal from ancient Chinese mythology."

She stared at the ugly figurine with a dragon's head, a horse's body and a unicorn's feet.

"It's supposed to have the ability to ward off evil spirits and bring happiness and good luck," he said. "The legend says Pixiu angered the Jade Emperor, so the Emperor gave him a slap on the buttocks, sealing Pixiu's anus. After that, gold, silver and jewelry could only go into his body and not come out. Fengshui masters believe Pixiu can turn disasters into good fortune."

"Whatever the legend, is it valuable?"

He turned the reddish-orange figure over in his hand. "I can't tell what it might be worth."

"I still don't get it. If some criminal wants this smuggled out of the country, why does he want it now?"

"That's what we need to figure out." He rolled the totem over and over. After placing the Pixiu on the berth, he took its picture with his phone. "Let's see what my client can tell us." He entered something on the phone's screen.

"Who is your client?"

"An art dealer in San Francisco. A rash of smuggled Chinese artifacts has shown up on his doorstep. He was fooled into buying one, and the artifact's owner claimed it. His insurance company covered his loss but cancelled his policy. His business is suffering." Evan looked at his phone.

"Have a signal yet?"

"No." He held it out for her to see. "What do you say? Will you help me look for this guy?" he asked.

"How do you propose we do that?"

"By making you visible and searching for your attacker on the train."

"That sounds dangerous."

"Less dangerous than waiting for the bastard to sneak up on us."

Her body tensed. "You think he'll come after the Pixiu again, don't you?"

"He won't give up, but if we have the upper hand, I can protect you."

In her experience, her father had protected her, standing by his only child no matter what. Other men in her life had looked after their own interests and not hers. Evan was a question mark. He could want the Pixiu for himself.

She liked to think she could take care of herself and didn't need protection, but heaven help her if she had to go it again with the Chinese brute. She wasn't prepared to risk that on her own.

She wrapped the Pixiu back in the tissue, pulled her purse out of the closet and paused before tucking the figurine into a bottom corner. "I know this has put me in danger, but I think I should hang on to it."

"Okay, for the time being." He pocketed the phone. A hint of a smile formed on his face. "I can keep my eye on both of you."

Evan looked so self-assured and handsome. Still, she worried. Would he be there when she needed him?

A half hour later, Sarah walked ahead of Evan through a full first-class car, clutching her shoulder bag to her body. Ambient light shone overhead. The high-backed passenger seats faced away from her. She glanced at each occupant as she passed and took a closer look at those who snuggled under blankets with their eyes closed or hovered under their reading lights. When someone stared back, she focused on the suitcases in the overhead racks to fight the urge to run away and hide.

Evan had said *visible*. That was an understatement. She was the featured item on the menu like a whole steamed cod on a dinner platter.

She paused at the entrance to the second car. A baby snoozed in a stroller. The girl, sweet-faced, had a pink bow in her ebony hair. Her lips curved upwards in peaceful innocence. Sarah would have been snuggled in her berth by now if the bully hadn't strong-armed her. She hurried through the car, paying less attention but noticing a woman's sweater with a Christmas tree pin. A tremulous smile formed on her lips at the familiar sign of the upcoming holiday, the one she intended to spend in San Francisco.

When she reached the third first-class car, the odor of fried food overwhelmed her and a sinking sensation settled in her belly. What if she saw her attacker? What would she do? What would Evan do? She needed to think, to assess her resources, to decide how far she could trust her compartment mate.

By the time she stepped into the dining car, she had no appetite.

Evan secured a table at the end of the car and said, "I want both of us to have full view of who comes and goes."

They sat across from each other. She faced a mirrored wall that was at his back and avoided staring at her own image. She was not at her most attractive. She had pulled her dark hair into a tight chignon at the nape of her neck and blotted the dark circles under her eyes with make-up to no avail. Her long work hours had left her looking exhausted, and the threat against her life had heightened her senses. She tried to see and hear everything around her all at once. She was on overload.

"Comfortable?" He flashed that crooked grin again.

She inhaled. Was she comfortable? No, but she nodded in the affirmative. Was it necessary to be polite? No, she was responding to his charm. Then, her stomach clenched. "What makes you think my attacker will show up?" she asked in a demanding tone.

"People do things you'd never expect."

"Unexpected things make me nervous." Under the table, she rubbed the bruises on one shin.

He fixed his gaze on her and said, "They make my business interesting."

"Interesting in what way?" Her voice rose a decibel.

"I do a lot of surveillance which can get boring. So a case like this engages me."

"Makes sense." She reined in her attitude and made an effort to focus on who came and went.

When the waiter arrived, Evan translated. She ordered the available white wine, hoping the alcohol would numb the ache in her shoulder, arm muscles and whatever else was out of whack.

"In honor of the Winter Solstice," Evan said, "they're serving assorted dumplings, savory and sweet."

"I'm familiar with dim sum. I'll eat what you order." Maybe food would help her jitters.

The waiter left, but two tables ahead, the mirror reflected the back of a man who had stood up—muscular, stocky, a head of thick black hair on his round head. Her mouth went dry, her throat tightened and her body froze in place. She had an urge to scream. When he turned around, she held back. His reflected features were all wrong.

"You look pale," Evan said. "Do you see someone?"

"I thought I—" she stammered. "No, nothing." She calmed her trembling hands out of sight, placing them in her lap. If only she could trust Evan, be sure he would help her get through this mess and back home. If only she could feel safe...

The waiter brought wine, bottled waters and steamers of dumplings. She sipped the bland wine that had not a single note of her favorite California Chardonnay.

The food gave off a strong scent of ginger and garlic. "I remember something," she said, "The guy who attacked me smelled of garlic, so he probably already had dinner."

"Possible, but we can't assume anything," Evan said in a flat business like tone. "I've learned what people do matters, but truth often hides in what people don't do. We must consider everything." He took a drink of water.

She was impressed despite her doubts. "You sound very professional." She swirled the white wine in her glass and took a sip.

"Even PI's have a philosophy." His eyes crinkled at the corners like those of a movie hero with mischief on his mind. "What else do you remember?"

She shut her eyes. "About my height, stubby fingers." When she opened them, she shook her head. "I want to enjoy my dinner. Let's talk about you."

"What about me?"

"Where did you learn Chinese?" she asked.

"Immersion school. My father thought Mandarin would prepare me for the future."

"Our fathers had the same idea." She mimicked a deep male voice. "German is the language of science."

He laughed out loud for the first time in a warm carefree way as if he were enjoying himself. "Did you study German?"

Animated by the joy he exuded, she sensed her muscles relax. "I went to Saturday classes. I considered going into medicine like my Dad but got interested in computers, so I studied biology and computer science at Berkeley. Ended up an Applications Specialist for hematology equipment."

"What exactly do you do?"

"I accompany equipment and teach techs how to use its software. What did you study?"

"Criminal Justice at San Francisco State. I followed in the old man's footsteps."

Her breath caught. "Are you from the city?"

"Grew up near Golden Gate Park and now have a bachelor pad adjacent in the Richmond area. And you?"

"I'm south of you in an apartment near the University of San Francisco."

"We're neighbors." He raised his water glass to her.

His lop-sided smile was definitely growing on her. He was in a bachelor pad—single. An eligible guy from her hometown. Geographically desirable. But did he have a girlfriend? What was she thinking? Of course, his availability would be a good question but later. Trust mattered more right now than her pipe dreams of finding a future with the right man.

She sighed. "I'm looking forward to getting home, walking around Union Square and seeing all the lights. I love the city at Christmas."

His phone pinged. He placed it on the glass tabletop. "It's from the auction house. They think the artifact valuable enough to protect and definitely want to test it once I get back." He slid her the phone.

Sarah took it and read the message. "What kind of value are we talking about?"

"Fifty, a hundred thousand before they get concerned."

"I didn't pay that kind of money for the plaster of Paris figure they never gave me." She chewed on her lower lip.

"What did you pay?"

"A couple of hundred Yuan," she answered.

"About $30."

Not even in the same ballpark as the Pixiu if what he was telling her was true. "Has your firm responded to the other e-mail we sent?" She needed confirmation from his employer. Was he who he claimed to be?

"Not yet, but they will." Lifting a dumpling with chopsticks, he leaned over the table and made eye contact. "Considering the potential value, it might be better if I held on to the Pixiu."

She pressed into the cushion at her back, her stomach hard as a rock. She wasn't about to give up the Pixiu until she was sure he was who he said he was. "It's safe in my purse."

"It has already put you in danger." He took a bite of the dumpling.

"It or you. I'm not sure which."

He swallowed his mouthful and looked down into his plate.

Damn! She didn't mean to say that. Now that she had, she couldn't take it back.

After her comment, they stopped talking. She picked at her dumplings, and he, without lifting his gaze, scarfed down several more of his. When she took her last sip of wine, he suggested they head back to their compartment.

Damn! Dinner resulted in a headache that stabbed behind her eyes. A bit of a rest on her berth might help.

At the compartment door, she stopped. Jagged slashes cut the composition fabric below the metal plate of the lock mechanism.

"What's wrong?" Evan asked from behind.

She pointed. He slid the door open a crack and looked inside, blocking her view.

"Is someone in there?"

"Not any more." He pushed the door aside.

"No," she mumbled.

The upper and lower berths sat open with their bedding stripped. Her clothing, scattered like dry leaves on a windy day, covered every surface. Her rolling bag, shredded, revealed its fiberglass frame. Her few personal items in the bathroom rolled on the floor. She opened her mouth to speak, but no words came.

Behind her, the door slid shut. "He's not giving up," Evan said.

Her head throbbed. Her heartbeat pulsed in her ears. Her privacy had been violated. Her personal belongings pawed by her horrible attacker. She placed her purse on the berth and picked up a white blouse. She then wrapped her underwear, bra, nightgown, and hose inside it. Clutching the bundle to her chest, she held back her urge to cry. What had she gotten herself into?

"I can't do this," she said, her voice shaky. "I don't feel safe, haven't since the attack."

From behind, gentle hands cradled her upper arms. She didn't hesitate to lean into Evan's broad chest, let his muscular body support her. His nearness sucked all the oxygen out of the compartment. The space seemed to shrink as if he was the only person on the planet who mattered.

"I know how unsettling this is," he whispered in her ear. "You've been victimized, but we can get through this together."

She inhaled a breath. Working with him would be easy. Still, her cautious nature needed assurance—confirmation of his identity. She turned around. "You can stay in the compartment with me, but I won't help you look for anyone."

"I'll settle for being your bodyguard," Evan murmured.

Mustering a hopeful tone, she said, "That's what I need." She needed much more, but at the moment, protection was as much involvement as she could afford without letting her guard down.

"At your service," he said with a hint of a bow. "Let's clean up?"

"Yes." As she placed the bundle on the armchair that was slashed across the back, his phone bleeped an incoming text.

"I think this is what you've been waiting for." He held it out.

Taking it, she read the confirmation of his employment. The tightness in her shoulders eased as if a weight had been lifted. "They even sent a photo of you standing in front of the company sign—Murphy International Intelligence."

"The *San Francisco Chronicle* used that in an article about an art recovery we made a couple of years ago." He bent to pick up a high-heeled shoe and examined it. "Nice. I'd like to see these on."

"I could probably arrange that." A hint of a smile sat on his lips, and Sarah felt an answering tug in her chest. "I grant you are who you say." A sense of relief flooded through her, and she handed over his phone. "I'm ready to listen. How can I get home safely?"

They made plans, deciding first to finish the cleanup and second to stay in the compartment until morning when they reached their destination, Shenzhen. Evan would contact the authorities he'd dealt with in the past to alert them and request assistance. He and Sarah would turn over the Pixiu, and she would be on her way to the Hong Kong airport to catch her flight home on schedule.

"The artifact will never leave China," Evan said. "It'll take some time to figure out why your attacker wanted the Pixiu before it went through customs."

"You'll let me know?"

"I have your card. I'll for sure email you. Least I can do after all you've been through."

Comforted by his words, Sarah arranged her belongings in stacks on the bottom berth they had made up.

He picked up her demolished suitcase. "Now, neither of us has luggage."

She laughed. "I'm better off. I at least have clothes."

"And I don't have to pack, wearing all I have." He moved close. "Do you have a scarf?"

She showed him the two she had brought, one a large square and the other a long rectangle.

Choosing the square, he laid it out next to her stuff. "I used my mom's tablecloths when I planned to run away from home." He piled a bunch of her things in the middle and tied the scarf crosswise hobo style.

Her gaze drifted to his capable hands with their long, lean fingers and neatly trimmed nails. The memory of those gentle hands as they'd comforted her warmed her cheeks. They were thrown together by circumstances, and she believed he was a nice guy. Apart from his job and where he lived, she knew little about him. Now, she wanted to know everything.

"Did you run away from home often?" she asked.

"I threatened, but I seldom made it out of the yard. My two brothers saw to that." He laughed in a heartfelt way.

"Your mother had her hands full."

"She still does even though we're adults." He laid out the second scarf. "I'm going to let you pack this one while I get us something to drink."

Her heart lurched. "I don't…"

"I'll be a minute. There's bottled water at the end of the corridor."

"Okay." She took a breath inward to fortify herself as he walked away.

She was ready to tie up the second scarf when the compartment's door shuddered and crashed open before crashing shut again. "Oh!" Sarah cried out with a ragged breath and took two jerky steps backward.

The man who had attacked her pushed Evan into the compartment from behind. He held a knife, its blade thick and silver, to her protector's throat.

"You give Pixiu, or I kill this devil." The goon addressed Sarah with a guttural tone in heavily accented English. She swallowed back the bile that rose in her throat.

Evan's eyes flared. He shook his head with a message that said *don't do it.*

She threw him an "are you crazy" stare but knew she had to buy him some time. She stalled. "I have to find it." Hands shaking, she fumbled around, shifting her shoes and the clothes tied in the scarf bundle.

"You hurry." The bully scraped the knife over Evan's skin.

Her pulse hammered. "Yes." She fished around in her purse. The Pixiu bundle sat in the bottom corner, but instead of picking it up, she removed the contents piece by piece—a wallet, hairbrush, tube of lipstick, pack of tissues, phone. By the time she produced a map of San Francisco, her attacker's face turned crimson.

"You give now," the guy growled. A vein in his temple pulsed as if it were ready to burst.

She mentally crossed her fingers and did what she did best. She placed her fingertips around the wrapped Pixiu and lifted it out. She threw it underhand. Within milliseconds, the perfect pitch made contact with the soft part of his temple where the vein throbbed.

He screamed. He dropped the knife and grabbed his head.

Evan straightened and jerked a knee up into the man's groin. Her attacker's face contorted. A gagging moan gushed from his throat. His body sagged. His hands cupped the injured flesh as he fell to the floor in a mound.

Evan produced some quick ties from a pant pocket. He moved with dexterity and speed to secure the brute's hands behind his back. He then held the goon by the shirt collar.

On wobbly legs, Sarah stumbled forward. Letting out a huge breath, she flopped into the armchair. The Pixiu sat at her feet still tightly wrapped. She picked it up. A spot of blood tinged one side of the tissue.

Evan now spoke in Chinese. She occasionally made out the word Pixiu and figured his harsh tone proved he meant business. Her attacker responded with wide-eyed quickness. When the conversation was over, Evan forced the man to sit on the floor in the small space.

"How are you doing?" Evan asked.

"I'm okay," Sarah said, a shaky chuckle in her tone.

"You were great." He pulled his phone from a pocket. "I'll explain what he said after I make a couple of calls."

She nodded. She shook her arms, releasing the tension in her muscles. Her heart pumped as if she'd worked out at the gym. A crazy sense of accomplishment filled her. She would be home for Christmas.

Pocketing his phone, he said, "Security will lock this bastard up until we get to Shenzhen."

Sarah stood and placed the Pixiu in her purse. "What did he say?"

"His name is Chen. The clerk at the gift shop accidently gave you the boxed Pixiu instead of the package you were supposed to smuggle. He then offered Chen a sizeable fee to get the Pixiu back any way possible before it left the train."

"And Chen knew just where to find me."

"How?"

"The clerk offered to deliver my purchase to my hotel, so I told him where I was staying. Then, I had second thoughts, and he said he'd wrap my souvenir for travel."

"Of course, the clerk had the package you were supposed to smuggle in the storeroom and somehow got the boxes mixed up."

"I took my souvenir out of its box to carry in my purse but never looked inside the wrapping. It was the right size and weight. They fooled me."

"Their business is to fool people."

"Does Chen know anyone else who is involved?'

"No, he claims he only knows the clerk." Evan shrugged. "He says he did it to pay off a gambling debt. My guess is he's telling the truth."

"What about the Pixiu?"

"The clerk instructed Chen to give the artifact to some men who are meeting him in Shenzhen. He'll still meet them but with me and a police escort in tow."

"What will you do with the Pixiu?"

"I'll turn it over to the authorities. I have a friend in the Public Security Bureau I've worked with in the past. We'll clear everything up, but it'll take a while." He smiled. "By the way, that's a great arm you have."

"I was a pitcher, high school varsity softball."

"We make a good team."

"Yes," she sighed. Evan had done as he promised, and in the end, they had protected each other.

She sat back down in the armchair. The train slid down the rails. The silence she had hoped for when she boarded enveloped the compartment.

━━━━━◆◆◆━━━━━

On December 22, Sarah opened her email folder. The first message that came in was from Evan. She took a deep breath and read, forming the words in a half-whisper.

"Am finally back. You'll be interested to hear the Pixiu dated to the reign of Emperor Qianlong in the 1700s, was priceless and stolen from a private collection in Paris."

She twisted her lips and chuckled. To think she had treated it like your ordinary softball and thrown it at someone.

She continued, "The authorities are seeing to its return to France. Can you meet for a drink tonight? I know—short notice. Union Square at seven. By the tree."

Could she ever! Yes, yes, yes.

She'd worried she would never hear from Evan. After her attacker was moved from their compartment, she fell asleep. When she woke, Evan had brought tea and bean buns for their breakfast. She grabbed a few bites of the doughy buns filled with a sweet paste while gathering her belongings. They barely had time to say goodbye. "I'll contact you," he had said before she rushed off to catch her flight home.

She read the email again. Union Square. Drinks. The San Francisco safe date. If things didn't go the way you hoped, the investment in time and money was small. She couldn't blame him for being cautious. They barely knew each other.

Her fingers skipped across the keyboard. "Seven at the tree." She pushed send.

Her computer announced the time as eleven o'clock. She had an hour before she met her parents for lunch—a short lunch. She would squeeze in a mani-pedi in the afternoon. Now, what would she wear? Evan had only seen her in black pants and a khaki T-shirt with her hair pulled into a bun at the nape of the neck. Hardly date wear.

In the evening, she put on a body hugging red dress—deep, sensuous red—that said stop, do not touch, and yet who could resist. She brushed her dark hair into loose curls that fell about her shoulders. She was ready at six—early—but ordered a cab anyway.

The ride from her apartment took thirty minutes instead of the usual twenty. She drummed her fingers on the armrest all the way. At Post and Powell, she stepped out into unseasonably warm air and placed her black jacket over an arm. She walked ahead toward the impossibly tall Christmas tree glittering with a million lights.

Nothing in the city said Christmas like Union Square. Cheerful holiday music floated in the air. People rushed in every direction, carrying bags loaded with packages. The ice rink glowed in the colors of the rainbow. Macy's blazed with brilliant wreaths on every window. On all sides, stores and hotels displayed illuminated decorations to celebrate the season. If holiday spirit was defined as bright, its life force lived here.

She caught sight of Evan in a navy suit and red tie. He was early too. She waved. He looked past her as if he didn't see her. Then his lips tilted into that lop-sided smile that tugged at her heart. He soon stood next to her.

"So glad you came."

"Me too. I mean…" She couldn't think of anything to say like an unsophisticated girl on a first date.

He laughed and put his arm around her waist. "You're gorgeous in red and taller than I remembered."

She leaned against him, raised a foot to show him she wore the heels he had admired on the train.

"They definitely look better on." He tucked her closer, started to walk across the Square.

She drew into his warmth, feeling snug and protected. "Where are we going?"

"How about dinner?"

"What happened to drinks?" They stopped for the streetlight.

The blue in his gunmetal eyes intensified as they met hers. "I need a lot of time with a woman who wears heels like those and can throw a softball."

She couldn't help smiling. "You can have as long as you want, but I have to explain about softball."

He put a finger to his lips. "Explain after you've seen my fastball."

"You play?"

"San Francisco Softball League."

When the light turned green, they stepped off the curb together, as one. The air was cool and crisp, the night full of promise.

When **Ottilia Scherschel**, a Hungarian immigrant, started sixth grade, she learned her fifth language. After retiring from teaching languages at the college level, she spends her time writing romantic suspense stories set in foreign climes. She has been a finalist in a number of writing contests and published a short story in the *Romancing the Pages* anthology. She has completed a novel set in China and is rewriting her second that is set in Hungary and Italy.

Ottilia loves to pack a suitcase to visit family, friends and food or wine purveyors anywhere in the world. When she is not writing, she can be found at the movies, at the gym, or cooking for her husband, kids and grandkids.

Winter's Warmth

by AK Shelley

Chapter One

Tim

Turning from the charts, Tim knocked the hollow scope twice for luck. Somewhere in that empty cylinder, he'd find a habitable planet. A perfect world.

Upsand beckoned him.

The radial velocities of the star Upsilon in the Andromeda constellation befuddled most extrasolar planet seekers. But when Tim added second and third planets beyond its Jovian-sized giant, the data nestled in an eccentric sine-wave. The math couldn't be wrong. The habitable planet had to be there. He simply hadn't found it. Yet.

He checked latitudes and longitudes, fiddled one dial and the other. Rechecked his notes. He released a held breath, barely registering the car door slam below. Its horn shocked his heart out of its peaceful rest. Mid-fall, he lurched away from the dials he'd been calibrating for the last twelve hours and landed on his rear on the observatory's stone floor.

The cab honked once more.

"*Christ.*" Tim swung open a panel window on the observatory. A yellow cab squatted in the drive, and a not-small woman walked up his front steps. "No solicitors!"

She lifted her face to meet his stare. Her mouth hung open for a moment. On second thought, she didn't look like she was selling anything. He could've asked her why she was here a tad more gently.

"What do you *want?*" That came out wrong. But surely everyone knew he had neither the time nor the desire to entertain.

They know. Your research is far too important. Send her away.

"I'm here to…" She narrowed her eyes at him and pulled something from her pocket. She waved a paper. "I need to know about this."

He needed his bloody telescope to see whatever she held. One of these days, he'd take the portable welder down to the gate and shut it permanently. It'd be hard to get his groceries delivered—but how long had it been since he had groceries delivered anyway? He couldn't remember. Food appeared when he needed it. It wasn't important.

He huffed. "I'll be right down."

The words came before he thought them. Of course he'd go to her. He pushed away from the desk and paced to the door.

The air in the converted attic froze. Ice spread across the floor—his breath caught in clouds. This house had the strangest weather.

Stop.

Below, the doorbell rang. His feet compelled him to move, following a memory he couldn't grasp. He hurried to the stairs.

The wind hissed through the window. *Sssstop!*

Tim shook his head. The visit was a minor inconvenience. He'd return to the scope after dismissing the woman. He grasped the doorknob. The brass froze in his hand, ice crackling in his palm.

He yanked his fingers away, red and burning. "*Jesus.*"

The searing pain released some pressure in his skull, and a strange clarity filtered through. *What was he doing here?*

Shhh, a crystalline finger grazed his nape. His newly found lucidity slowed, muddied. That hiss in his mind alien, not his—

Go back to your scope. She'll leave on her own.

She always does.

The doorbell rang once again, echoing through the hallway below.

A glacial gust slapped his chest. He glanced around the room, half convinced he'd see a familiar companion there. Only an empty, cold space met his gaze. He kicked the crystals away and folded his sweater sleeve around his fingers before grappling the door open.

Somewhere far below, a feminine voice called. "Hello?"

Sweetness and light and home infused that one simple word. Tim took one look behind him, frost spreading at his feet, and ran downstairs.

The frigid air followed him into the long hall, sweeping through the sprawling ballroom, smaller dining room and lounges. Fingers of frost grasped at his heels as he ran for the door.

Return to the telescope. You must find the planet. His thoughts were insistent, his house freezing.

It was always cold in here, wasn't it? He'd light some fires after the girl went away.

You won't need them. All by yourself in the observatory, it'd be a waste to light the fires in the empty rooms below.

True, he supposed. After the woman left, he'd return to his work.

"Hello?"

The warmth, softness of her voice cut through the rime, through his obsessions, arresting everything in a present warmer, comforting, accepting. Familiar. Like home. Like love.

He turned a corner and found her standing barely in the foyer, wind gusting around her bundled form. Wisps of long dark hair escaped her furry hood, her breath puffs of smoke.

"Alma." He didn't know her name, but it came to his tongue with familiar disappointment. Images, memories jumbled. She left him alone here. *She came back.* He blinked.

Her cheeks flushed red, her lips like roses. She opened them, but no words followed. Her dark brown eyes large, framed in feathery black lashes.

"Tim?" she whispered.

Wind, shrill and frigid, howled though the doorway, down the hall. Alma hugged herself.

"Come." His arms, familiar somehow with her body, wrapped around her shoulders. He guided her away from the foyer, outside where the air was somehow less frigid.

Her arms, warm and strong under her woolen coat. A fiery heart beat within. Not many women came fully to his height. How did he know that? Family, and other women flitted past his recollection in wisps of memory.

His muscles loosened, a funny warmth spreading, melting inside. Like she shone a beam of sunlight into his heart. He found himself smiling for no particular reason, his weariness evaporating. She was a force of her own.

"Do you know where this came from?" She paused at the bottom of the stairs. Her brown eyes sparkled, but her eyebrows pulled together.

The paper she'd waved pressed into his hand. The card—for it was clear now that is what she'd waved at him—showed a Christmas scene with a sled and cheery mistletoe *and his house.* Unlike the actual building, looming angles and sharp corners and dominating the sleeping mountain behind it. The mansion in the card burrowed merrily under a veil of holiday spirit.

"Never saw it before." He glanced behind him to windows crusted with ice. "This is the same house, though I can't say how this was painted." He shrugged. "I haven't had guests since…"

He shook his head, a memory flitting before his eyes. Alma, dressed in a full-skirted dress and lace-lined bonnet, a horse-drawn carriage waiting where the cab now stood. Shock stood plainly on her face, and the cold emptiness settling in once more. Claws of ice clutched at his heart.

She left before, and she'll leave again.

"I got this…" Alma squinted and tilted her head in a familiar way. "…a few days ago." She closed her eyes. "I'm sure I've gotten them before…"

She motioned for him to open the card.

One word marked the inside.

Come.

Written in his handwriting.

But he'd never seen the card before, and he didn't know this woman. Did he? *And how did he know her name?* Memories drifted past his reach. She'd been here before. And a time before. Yet—no. He'd been alone. Always alone. Alone with the house.

The cabbie honked. Face flushed, the driver rolled down the passenger window. "Are you staying? 'Cause I got a fare waiting."

Whatever spell the woman had on him broke. He had to get back to work. Whoever she was, he didn't have time for her. He held out his hand to shake hers, and stamped a polite but firm good-bye smile on his face.

She hesitated before taking his hand, squishing her lips into a line. "Oh well. Thanks for, uh, coming down."

Somewhere above, a crack shattered the air. A low groan followed. *She needs to go now.* The cabbie laid on the horn, gesturing madly at the tower above.

Leave her. Leave them both.

Before realizing what he was doing, his feet walked up the stairs toward the door. He stopped and blinked, trying to clear the inexplicable mud in his brain. Unthinking, he gripped Alma's hand and glanced up.

The supports for his satellite dish twisted in a strange, almost graceful pirouette. Alma gasped. Adrenaline rushed through his veins.

She would not take Alma away again. Not so permanently. He pulled her away from the house, towards the car.

A half second later, the dish plummeted. It crashed on the stairs, cracked in two, in a nest of frozen metal and fiberglass shards. Right where Alma had been standing.

Chapter Two

Alma

100% AUTHENTIC TROLL MIRROR FRAGMENTS. GUARANTEED!

Alma rolled her eyes at the glittery display, and hmphed at the subdued crowd in the tiny convention room beyond. The sooner she got out of this town, the better. She peered out of the hotel foyer's windows, hazy with cold and snow. The cab company said the car would be here ten minutes ago. She sighed.

Crystals clinked into the pottery bowl. A 70s-something woman with a shock of blue-black hair watched her under smoky-lidded eyes. Anyone could see the kook peddled ordinary crystals. Definitely not troll mirror fragments. Whatever *those* were.

Before she left this little Northern Idaho town, she needed to find something for the museum. So Martin would take her back. So the unusual visit—right before his new exhibit opened on January 1st—wouldn't be a bust.

Her body shivered in the shock of her first winter outside of Southern California. She'd come to uncover the mystery behind those Christmas cards. But the most obvious source—the actual mansion on the cards—was a false lead. That man was not the type to send holiday greetings.

Tim.

Did she actually know him? Her amnesia, chronic and dogged as a perpetual shadow, clouded the past. He was strangely familiar. The strength in his arms when he wrapped them around her, leading her from the house. That quizzical look he gave when she handed the card to him, so familiar she could imagine his thoughts behind his dark eyes. The way his lips took a funny little banana shape when they quirked up. She could almost taste them. The love—surprising, that was what she felt—when he pulled her to his chest and away from the falling satellite dish. When he saved her life.

And the ice that claimed his eyes when he dismissed her. The cold house reflected in his heart.

Alma shivered. It was like she'd lived the day before.

But she hadn't expected to be met with a psychic convention when she rolled her bag downstairs. She fiddled with the corner of the card in her pocket. "What are... troll mirror fragments?"

The elderly woman rubbed her hands, settling in to a good story. "Long ago a troll—which is just an old way of saying *devil*," she leaned forward and whispered, as if in conspiracy, "smashed the goddess Freya's mirror and scattered the shards across the world. These are amethyst."

She sifted a handful of crystals through her fingers and smiled. "Besides stories and crystals, I can also tell your fortune. Got the sight, powerful. None of those demons whispering in my ears. Got the divine power."

Alma bit her lip. This conversation was more than she bargained for. She searched the room for something artifact-like. Something for the museum.

The woman cleared her throat. She painted on polite patience. "What brings you to our little town?"

Locals flipped through displays of tarot and meandered by tables of semi-precious jewelry and a large corner display of crystal balls. She'd never find anything for Martin here. Which meant until the taxi arrived, talking to the woman couldn't be avoided.

"I'm here to find out who sent me this." Alma pulled out the card. "Do you know the artist?"

The psychic raised an eyebrow. "Let's have a chat." She pulled out a chair next to hers and motioned for Alma to take it. "So, what broke the spell?"

"Spell?" Alma felt her polite smile falter. She wasn't under any spell.

"I can still see remnants of it." The woman furrowed her brows as she studied Alma's face. "Definitely a spell. You have memory problems?"

Alma rubbed the cold off her arms. The world of museum deals and the acquisition of ancient treasures shimmered, a mirage. The life she led in Los Angeles splintered into a thousand shards. "I..."

She nodded. Memories bubbled beyond recollection. Her stomach hardened as she tried to still her hands. She shook nonetheless. She sought for more than the card's sender. She'd been searching for longer than she could remember. "I started to remember when I found this rose."

She pulled the hearty, thick stemmed flower from the pocket where it lay pressed against her heart. Since yesterday, the bloom had been a source of comfort. Her thoughts cleared with its scent. The flushed petals trembled as she held it out to the old woman.

Her abrupt departure was spurred by the blood red rose she found in the museum gardens the day before. The blossom oddly glowed in that golden afternoon light. She'd brought the flower to her nose and was blanketed in scent and memory. She knew, *knew*, she was supposed to be somewhere else. She was supposed to be at the mansion in her mysterious Christmas card.

Martin tried to stop her, of course. Begged her to stay, said she was his best artifact hunter. Cursed her for leaving before his new exhibit opened. What would he do without her? A puzzle, the man she'd worked for for so many years was a stranger, the life she'd been living wrong. She sped away from the museum, packed a hurried bag, and took the next flight to Sun Valley, Idaho. Left before she forgot, again.

"Your destiny is here. Doubt not." The old woman nodded, like she'd heard every thought. She smiled knowingly at the rose and flicked the card. "There've always been rumors about that mansion. Of course, no one realizes he's her captive."

Alma held her breath. Something about the way the woman spoke told her she needed to hear more. Desperately. "Tim's... a captive?"

"The Ice Queen's." The woman rolled her eyes. "She's been here as long as the mansion. Came from the homeland, stories say."

The old psychic surveyed the tables around them. "You need to go back," she said, tapping the Christmas card.

Alma sighed. "He doesn't want me there."

"You *must* return. Don't leave without him. If you do, you'll wander again. You'll wander endlessly. That memory problem of yours? It'll come back. Worse, this time. Such is the nature of her curse." The woman grasped Alma's wrist, her hand bony, papery, warm. "But heed me: Her power has grown in your absence. She is preparing for something new. Ready yourself to fight. She'd sooner see him dead than let him go."

━━◆━━

The cabbie drove in silence up the long stretch of abandoned road. Twenty minutes into the drive, he turned onto the familiar thin driveway overhung by fir trees crowding the road. A brick formed in Alma's gut. The cab stopped at the old iron gate that spanned the driveway.

"You want me to drive you all the way to the house?" he said. "It'll be an extra five bucks."

"Yeah, that's fine." The house was a ten-minute drive from the gate. Did he expect her to walk in this weather?

He grunted as he leaned back to accommodate his girth, and climbed out of the car to swing the gate open, as he'd done the day before. Freezing air gusted through. Alma shivered and pulled her hood over her head.

She should have left for LA, but a psychic at a little fair convinced her of some destiny and like a fool she believed it. Yet somehow, these woods resonated with her. Somehow, the words the woman spoke rang true. Alma slipped the rose from an inner pocket and smoothed a petal across her fingertip. Its absorbing, reminiscent fragrance confirmed it. She was meant to be here.

If only she could remember her past.

The cab driver paced toward the iron bars and fiddled with the chain.

In the 24 hours she'd been away from the museum, she'd noticed her head was less fuzzy. She felt more herself than she had in years. Why had leaving been such a big deal for Martin, when she was one of several associate curators?

Outside, the driver dropped the chain and returned to the vehicle. He grumbled about tourists as he dumped himself back into the driver's seat.

"Sorry," he said. "Gate's welded shut."

Finally, a real reason to turn around and go home. But instead, the immovable gate settled her choice like a boulder in her chest. She had to get to Tim. At the very least, to see he was alright.

She handed the man a fifty and pulled on her gloves. "I'll get out here."

Chapter Three

Together

Alma squinted into the icy wind, bundled against the cold. The mansion stood quiet and dark, same as yesterday.

The satellite dish had been dragged off the stairs and laid on its side against the smooth, white stone building. The stairs where the equipment hit had crumbled, and several large cracks emanated from the impact crater.

Alma let out a gust of breath. If she'd stood there a second longer, she'd be dead. She dashed up the remaining steps, fearful of what else might come from above.

Inside the shelter of the stoop, the house itself radiated cold. Alma raised her red glove, lifting the brass knocker on hollow frozen door.

No answer came.

She pushed the bell.

Somewhere within, a chime tinkled like shattering glass. Still, no sound betrayed that anyone heard her summons.

She took a deep breath to ready herself.

Memories came easier now, easier than they had in years. She *had* been here before. Once in a Model T. Once before that in a carriage. Once on horseback. Every time, this ice, this cold. Every time, she'd lost him to her. The Ice Queen.

The door would be unlocked, as before. Something about the house, cold and relentless, stood above threat. It had no need for locks. Alma pushed the front door open and stepped inside.

She'd find out what happened to her, to him, or she'd never know. Restless past and futures taunted her. She'd never remember the past, and be forced relive it again and again. Just like the old psychic told her. Like falling down a well without end.

Unsteadily, she treaded down frozen carpet runner, following the hallway stretched before her. Blue-white patches of light filtered in through adjoining rooms. She recognized more of the house, its silvery chandeliers, the expansive ballroom sheeted in ice like a skating rink.

Frost climbed her coat as she neared a set of stairs. Tim should have met her by now, and under the spell of the Ice Queen, would be ushering Alma to the door. Wrongness filled the cavernous space. She had to hurry.

Tim would be in the observatory. The ghost would stop her from reaching him, if she could. Alma ran, taking two steps at a time.

The wind howled around her. It gusted across a landing, pushing her into the rickety banister.

How dare you? Gloom in the corners thrust disembodied words at her.

Across Alma's chest heat spread. She reached into an inner pocket, touching the warm red rose there. The house crowded with familiar memories. Time and time before she'd come to take Tim away. And failed. She would not fail again.

"I dare because I must," Alma said between breaths. She sprinted the last few steps to the observatory.

He's mine! The spirit hissed.

The door froze in its frame.

Alma raised her heavy boot and kicked the wooden panel in.

A wall of arctic air met her.

Tim sat huddled under a heavy coat at the telescope, peering into its lens. He didn't move.

"Tim?" Alma ran to his side.

The floor crunched under her feet, and the air matched the sound.

You're too late, the ghost cackled.

Between his scarf and his tuque, his skin showed the blue of a robin's eggshell.

"No." The rock lining her stomach fell. She crumpled to her knees beside him. "No, no, no."

She swiveled his seat to face her. His boots skidded across the floor.

The air chimed with laughter. *Too late, he's mine, too late.*

Alma tugged his scarf away, pushed his hood back. His eyes pale, unblinking, eyelashes encrusted with ice.

She whimpered. All those times she'd come for him, allowed him to turn her away, to convince her that the Ice Queen was what he wanted. Heat washed over her. She'd end the demon that took him.

Hands shaking, she pulled off a bright red glove and brushed his cheek. This would be their final goodbye. Under her fingers, his skin warmed, turned pink. A wisp of breath escaped his lips.

Alma gasped.

She gripped his cheeks in her hands, and her warmth spread across to his nose. He inhaled deeply. His pale skin deepened with an inner glow as her warmth reached past his forehead. His eyelashes melted, and he blinked his amber eyes.

"Alma?" a whisper escaped his lips white as death.

Her heart leapt. She pressed her mouth to his.

———

As kisses go, this one, perhaps, had the longest time coming.

Warmth spread first, down and through Tim's body. He hadn't even realized how very cold he'd been. Numb to feeling. Her lips, soft and warm, and sweet with the faint taste of cinnamon and… rose. He met her kiss, pressing his lips to hers.

The room around them fell silent.

In that void, heat exploded. Sparks of light coursed through him. He wrapped his arms around her and lifted her to his lap. Alma smiled, and pressed her lips to his once more. He suckled her luscious lower lip like a starving man.

The layer of ice around the scope began to drip on the floor, splashing in a tiny puddle. Everything he'd been missing, everything he searched for in the skies, was here. All those centuries long, it was Alma he longed for. Her love.

The Ice Queen tricked him. Convinced him that his world was poisoned, mad, filled with hatred. That to find what he sought, he needed to look to the cold emptiness of space. In her icy embrace, she'd nearly killed him.

Alma nuzzled his neck. Her warm breath tickled his ear as she whispered. "You okay?"

"I will be." His heart sped at the intimate connection. His solitude evaporated. He wrapped his arms around her, pulling her closer. She was all he needed, and more.

She tilted her head, listening. He couldn't help but smile. The expression brought back so many memories of her.

"We can't stay," she said.

He nodded. Even if the spirit haunting this house was quiet, they weren't safe. At least her spell was broken.

Tim stood, lifting Alma with him. If she was the sun, he was a tree, constantly reaching for her light. He breathed her in and set her on her feet. He grasped her hand.

"Let's go." He'd wanted to say those words for ages. Giddiness bubbled inside as they crossed to the door hanging askew on one hinge.

Oh, but you cannot leave your notebook. You'll lose all your work, when you were close to finding a second Earth. Get the book, for you will not return. You'll join her in a moment.

Tim's gut clenched. He couldn't lose everything he'd done. He'd made breakthroughs. He'd been meticulous in his notes.

Alma's eyes widened as he dropped her hand. She stopped on the other side of the threshold. "Tim?"

"Just one thing. I'll be right back." He ran to the table, shuffling papers. His notebook should be here. It was always here.

Hairs stood on his nape as the air around him cooled. He ignored it. He had to find his book. Then he could leave.

"Tim?" Alma's voice was more distant, somehow.

There… the leather cover wedged between the desk and the wall, hovering inches above the floor. He leaned over a mess of papers, reaching down.

Somewhere, someone pounded on a door, a wall.

He grasped the heavy leather spine and hauled it up. Pages flipped, some filled with illegible scribbles, others blank. A wave a sickness rolled over his stomach as his eyes passed over page after page of nonsense. Where were his notes? His breakthroughs? His breath clouded.

He had to get to Alma.

He dropped the book and turned to the doorway. She stood, pounding and screaming, on the other side of a thick wall of ice.

The air crackled with laughter.

"No!" He ran for the doorway, but his steps slowed with each movement. Ice clung to his boots. He grunted, pulling his feet away from the floor. Cold pulled at his fingertips, his ears, his eyes.

"Come now," a haughty voice whispered in his ear. "We can be together. Happy."

The familiar voice, he realized, the one in his thoughts. The one that wasn't his.

"No!" Tim threw himself at the ice. At least six inches thick, the wall continued to grow.

On the other side, Alma's face grew hazy. Wielding a splintered banister, she beat the wall with determination.

He'd been a fool to go back for the notes. Nothing here was worth saving.

He turned from the doorway. If he could get a window open, perhaps he could escape.

Before him stood a tall, graceful woman in a flowing crystalline robe. A delicate crown of ice adorned her long white hair. She'd have been breathtaking, if her eyes hadn't been frozen thick with cruelty.

A stone settled in Tim's gut. "You."

"Yes. Me." The Ice Queen smirked.

She leveled her gaze and swept a circle around him. Fingers of ice grazed his chin, his neck, his arms.

"How could you, Timothy?" Her sing-song voice beckoned him to entrance. "Leave me, after all I've given you?"

She pouted, flourishing her arm. The mansion. The observatory. The forest beyond. All his. Because it was hers.

"Could you abandon your work, after all you've done?"

A chill spread across his skin. This couldn't be happening. The warmth of Alma's kiss still heated his lips. He would not fall under the queen's spell again. Not this time.

"You are wrong, about this world. About us." He struggled to raise his boots off the floor.

"Wrong?" She leaned in, her body a vacuum drawing his heat away. "I fear not."

But in his chest, heat spread. His hand drew to the warmth and pulled out a single red rose. A clouded recollection of Alma slipping the flower into his coat.

The queen flinched.

"You have perfection, but it is lifeless. It is loveless. It is empty." The thorny stem burned in his palm, and he thrust it into the Queen's chest.

The flower burst into flames. She screamed and scratched at the rose to no avail. The flames spread, burning through her. The Ice Queen disappeared in a cloud of mist and smoke.

Through clouds of steam, a voice tugged at him. Warm hands pulled his sleeve. "Tim. We've got to go."

His boots loosened. He spun and caught Alma in his arms, planting fresh kisses on her lips. He'd never leave her side again.

Chapter Four

Alma

Splashes of red on the floor caught Alma's eye. Rose petals lay shattered and half burnt at their feet.

"She's gone." Tim let out a gust of breath. "Finally."

Alma glanced around the room. Everywhere, water dripped. Ice receded into corners, across window panes to their edges. The room lost its frosty tinge.

It was over. All the missing memories were replaced. She and Tim had been cursed centuries ago, worlds in time and miles away in Norway. And she'd wandered since, falling prey to minor spell and manipulations all because of the Ice Queen's magic.

The rose stem glinted. Alma bent to pick it up. The flower bud had burnt off. A blackened blade sleeved in thorns remained.

"How do we know?" she whispered.

Tim caressed her cheek. "Know what, my love?"

"That she's gone."

"She's got to be. The flames… she disappeared…"

Tim's chair crashed to its side. He paled. Gripping Alma's hand, he ran for the stairs.

Behind them, another object struck to the floor. Glass shattered, tinkling. That would have been his scope. He shoved the pang in his heart aside. There was more life for him beyond these walls. Much more.

The rose stem in Alma's hand steamed and hissed against the cool air. The frigidity of the house evaporated, its perpetual frost melting. But a cold darkness lurked in the shadows.

"Too weak to manifest." His last thoughts voiced themselves. "But she's still here. I can feel it."

Alma stopped on the ballroom threshold. Patches of ice melted into puddles across the once-intricate wood floor.

"She'll rise again," she said. "We must finish her."

He only wanted to leave this place. But more than anything else, he never wanted to be under the Ice Queen's spell again. Tim nodded.

Darkness crept along the corners of the hallway, flitted between window panes in the room beyond. Threats whispered beyond hearing.

"The rose stopped her upstairs," he started.

Alma fingered the stem's sharp edge. It pricked her skin easily, drawing blood. "Perhaps it will again."

Alma held a strength of light and warmth. And the flower held powers of its own. Had it come from the angels to save them, or was it a manifestation of love?

"Together," he said. "It must be both of us."

He paced to the middle of the ballroom, where the wood floor now lay bare and dry. They knelt together.

E

Thorns pierced their palms as they gripped the stem together, forming lines of a word driven by the rose.

T

The wood floor gouged easily under the stem.

E

The floor around the letters hardened to a shiny rock.

R

A shadowy filament pierced the wood around the letters, staining the petrified wood.

N

Blackness gathered above them from all corners and openings to the room, swirling into a vortex.

I

The shadows poured into the word. A slow, low wail built around them.

T

The sound heightened to a screech, shattering the windows overlooking the mountain above.

Y

The house fell silent, save for their gasping breaths. Sunbeams streamed through the empty windows, filling the room with brilliant light.

———◆———

Tim chuckled and set down his whiskey-ed coffee. On Alma's tablet, he pointed to what appeared to be the middle of the South Pacific. "There. I want to get as far from here as possible."

The warm candlelight sparked amber tones in his eyes. Alma sighed into this new feeling. She was pretty sure it was bliss. "Of course. We can go anywhere."

A classical version of "O Tannenbaum" rang through the hotel's sound system. Turned out, Christmas Day was the best time to catch a last-minute flight anywhere. Who would've guessed?

"But your house…" Alma didn't want to go back there either, but Tim couldn't abandon it.

He shrugged. "I'll call a real estate agent. Sell it."

"What if the Ice Queen comes back?" She bit her lip.

He quirked a smile. "She's gone, locked away. I can feel it."

Across the room, a large table, an extended family with children, parents, and grandparents, made Oohs and Aahs as a little girl and boy unwrapped two large boxes. Her long white dress and his little red bow tie stoked distant memories. Traditions from a time long ago. Alma smiled. This was a good time to be alive. To be together.

He nodded at the table. "The whole town can feel it. She's gone."

It was true. Everyone shone with merriness, far beyond the seasonal expectations of cheer. Even the cabbie had replaced his disgruntled mask with rosy cheeks and a belly laugh.

She and Tim left the mansion immediately after sealing the Ice Queen away, Alma calling back the cab with her cell. They'd warmed themselves with showers and food at the hotel, and spent the night with a giant Christmas tree and carolers on the town square. Despite the winter and the snow, this Christmas Eve was a night of warmth, light, and hope.

Like her and Tim's future.

"So, Fiji?" A warm beach and notable lack of clothing sounded like just what she needed.

"First, I have a request." He took her hand, his eyes glistening as he gazed into hers. "Marry me, Alma."

A.K. Shelley, a Canadian-Californian, former Buddhist nun and biologist, and all-around tree hugger, is the author of the middle-grade fantasy series Ennara and a two-time silver medalist at the Moonbeam Children's Book Awards. She spends her days wrangling twin Scorpios, avoiding social media (and sometimes succeeding), and penning tales of steely heroines and time travelling rogues.

Authors' Notes

We hope you enjoyed reading *Love for Christmas*. We all enjoyed writing it and hope it added the warmth of love to your holiday.

Please consider leaving a review of this book at the site where you purchased it since reviews are the best way for other readers to discover new books. We'd love it if you would like to share your thoughts.

Visit www.writingsomethingromantic.com, to learn more about all of the authors who contributed to this anthology, as well as to post your thoughts and comments.

You can also visit the following additional author websites to subscribe to their newsletters and get more information about other releases:

Kathleen Harrington at www.kathleenharringtonbooks.com

A.K. Shelley at www.akshelley.com

Jill Jaynes at www.jilljaynes.com

Made in the USA
Las Vegas, NV
28 July 2021